The Face of Deceit

RAMONA RICHARDS

D0210202

Steeple
Hill®

Published by Steeple Hill Books™

STEEPLE HILL BOOKS

Steeple
Hill®

ISBN-13: 978-0-373-44307-9
ISBN-10:   0-373-44307-2

THE FACE OF DECEIT

www.SteepleHill.com

Printed in U.S.A.

"I started having nightmares about being chased," Karen said.

"I couldn't tell who it was," she added, "but there was *this* face." She tapped the photo of her vase again. "I woke up in such a panic that I..." She swallowed. "I'd never felt a fear like that. I did the first vase in an attempt to get rid of the nightmare. I never expected to sell it—or that it would be the start of dozens of others."

"Any idea what the dream meant?" Mason asked.

She frowned. "You mean, like an interpretation?"

"Sure. Remember that the Bible is full of dreams and visions, and most meant something significant." Mason paused and shoved his hands into his pockets, a little puzzled by his own words. Where had that come from? He knew the Bible, but not much beyond a childhood Sunday-school level. "What if your memory is picking up on someone you really know and plopping it on those vases?" he asked.

Karen turned to him. "It can't be."

"Why not?" If her dreams were a memory trying to work its way out, this was the logical response, the only response. He swallowed hard, dropping his voice. "Karen, has anyone ever tried to kill you?"

Karen's eyes met his, evenly, solidly. "Yes."

Books by Ramona Richards

Love Inspired Suspense

A Murder Among Friends
The Face of Deceit

RAMONA RICHARDS

A writer and editor since 1975, Ramona Richards has worked on staff with a number of publishers. Ramona has also freelanced with more than twenty magazine and book publishers and has won awards for both her fiction and nonfiction. She's written everything from sales training video scripts to book reviews, and her latest articles have appeared in *Today's Christian Woman, College Bound* and *Special Ed Today.* She sold a story about her daughter to *Chicken Soup for the Caregiver's Soul,* and *Secrets of Confidence,* a book of devotionals, is available from Barbour Publishing.

In 2004, the God Allows U-Turns Foundation, in conjunction with the Advanced Writers and Speakers Association (AWSA), chose Ramona for their "Strength of Choice" award, and in 2003, AWSA nominated Ramona for Best Fiction Editor of the Year. The Evangelical Press Association presented her with an award for reporting in 2003, and in 1989 she won the Bronze Award for Best Original Dramatic Screenplay at the Houston International Film Festival. A member of the American Christian Fiction Writers and the Romance Writers of America, she has five other novels complete or in development.

Ramona and her daughter live in a suburb of Nashville, Tennessee. She can be reached through her Web site, www.ramonarichards.com.

In the morning, O Eternal One, listen for my voice; in the day's first light I will offer my prayer to You and watch expectantly for Your answer.

—*Psalms* 5:3

To Sunny,
who first put me on a wheel
and let me disappear into the clay.
Your unparalleled friendship is a true blessing.

* * *

With special thanks to Vickie C. Martin
and her team at Goodlettsville, Tennessee's
Scentaments,
for the first drops of inspiration
for Karen's "face vases."

* * *

"Before you do anything else,
before you center it on the wheel,
before you think about what you're going to make,
listen to the clay. God created it;
it's part of His world.
Honor it. Honor Him.
Listen closely.
The clay has a voice. It has a memory.
It will tell you all you need to know."

—Jake Abernathy
Lessons to a Young Potter, 1989

ONE

"Not again!"

Karen O'Neill stared at the pottery shards clustered at the base of the open door, a twinge of fear tightening her chest. Her sudden words, although barely more than a whisper, startled the cat in her arms. The gray velvet half-Persian leaped free in a graceful arc over the threshold and disappeared into the hedges bordering the backyard.

"Lacey!" Karen stepped over the remains of the ceramic vase, her sense of fear escalating. "Wait!"

No good. The cat, cooped up all morning as Karen worked in her pottery studio, wasn't listening. "As if you ever do," Karen muttered. She quickly scanned her sloping, tree-covered backyard, searching for any signs of danger, any other human presence…any indication of who could have smashed a vase against her back door.

Karen's own vase, in fact. One of her own unique "face vases," a design she had first created a few years ago. Slender and marked by a distinctive white face on one side, the vibrantly colored vases had become her artistic trademark. Recently, they had become in-creasingly popular among galleries and collectors in the Northeast, a trend predicted by art historian Mason DuBroc, who had published an article on them. Mason, intrigued by the vases, had warned Karen that she needed to increase her output, to prepare for growing popularity. *"Everyone will love them,"* he'd insisted.

Someone, however, had taken a distinct dislike to the vases. A violent dislike.

Around her, the yard remained silent, revealing no clues. The only motion was from the prowling cat and a squirrel annoyed by the Persian's presence. Even the pink and gold flowers near the door, their heady scent lured out by the warm May sun, showed no indication of a breeze or a passing human. No lurking villains, no suspicious shadows. Peaceful.

Except for the shattered vase. The third vase this month. Karen hadn't ever heard a crash, making her think the attacker knew when she was in the house and when she was not. As a result, Karen fought a feeling of being stalked. Watched.

She shivered despite the warmth of the spring sun, then scolded herself. *You're just being paranoid.* She pushed the thought away and turned back to the door, bending to look closer at the remains of the vase, careful not to touch any of the pieces. Yep, there it was, as with the other two—the scrap of paper, weighted down by one of the larger shards, that read simply, Stop!

"Stop what?" She straightened and stepped over the vase into her basement studio, still talking to herself. "Stop making vases? Stop *these* vases? Stop pottery altogether?"

Karen froze at the idea, looking around, her gaze moving from her shelves of pottery supplies, to the worktables, to the wheel. She could no more give up pottery than walk on the moon. Pottery wasn't just something she did. It was her life. It had *saved* her life.

She took a deep breath. "Lord, give me strength," she whispered, then headed up the narrow, wrought-iron spiral steps that led from her studio to her living room. Time to call the police. Again.

"Vandalism? That's it? After three vases!" The barely restrained anger in the dark male voice on the other end of the phone gave Karen an odd sense of comfort. She had been tense when she'd called the police, but now she relaxed as she leaned back against her couch cushions and stretched her legs. Lacey, who'd scratched at the front door to get in almost as soon as Karen had come upstairs, sensed the change in mood. She leaped into Karen's lap and started kneading one thigh, sharp claws pricking through Karen's jeans.

Karen stroked Lacey idly, focusing on the voice in the phone. Mason DuBroc had become a good friend over the past few months, since his arrival in town. Well-known in the art community as half art professor and half adventurer, Mason had been the last person she'd expected to find on her doorstep one dreary January morning. Karen had read his articles and books, had followed stories about him in the press. Mason was art world A-list, and she'd reacted as if a Hollywood star had been standing there. She had stared, openmouthed, at the disheveled man, snow clinging to his floppy hat and weathered hiking boots, his questions flying at her faster than she could answer them. Now Karen found herself wondering if his deep brown eyes flashed as much in anger as they did in excitement.

"There's not much else the local police can do, Mason. The Stop! isn't really a threat, and they couldn't find any fingerprints. They consider it in the same way they would if someone had spray-painted the house."

A low growl echoed through the phone, and with each word, Mason's Cajun accent thickened. "But this isn't a prank. They didn't spray-paint the house. They destroyed art! *Your* art! Don't they think someone's watching you?"

Karen closed her eyes and curled her fingers in Lacey's fur. She didn't really want to face that possibility. "They are going to patrol the neighborhood more often, but with the woods that start at the edge of the yard and go for miles, there's not much they can do. They only have five patrol officers."

"Almost wish I wasn't in New York. Maybe you should stay—"

"I'm not going back to Aunt Evie's, Mason." A touch of Karen's tension returned. "We talked about this the first time."

"Yes, but—"

"Absolutely not."

Karen held her breath. Mason knew all too well how tense her relationship was with the aunt who had raised her. They had battled since Karen's teen years, and now her choice of career made her aunt annoyed and critical.

"What about Jane? She's your best friend."

"I'm allergic to her dog."

Silence.

"Mason, I don't want to be forced out of my home. I worked too hard to make it my own."

Mason broke the thick silence that followed by

clearing his throat. "*Chère,* the auction starts this afternoon at three. If it goes as I hope, your profile will be even higher in the art world. Are you ready for that? More orders? More attention?" He paused. "Maybe more broken vases?"

Karen looked down as Lacey settled in for a nap, her purr a soft vibration under Karen's fingers. Karen, too, felt calmer. *Chère.* He'd started calling her that a few weeks ago, pronouncing it "Sha," and using it mostly when they were alone. She wasn't sure what it meant, but every time he said it, she felt herself relax. "Yes," she softly. "More orders, yes."

"And the attention?"

Lacey's breaths became light and even, her back barely rising and falling under Karen's hands. The young potter looked around at her cozy living room. Her adored hillside house, with its narrow three stories, barely contained a thousand square feet. Yet it was something she'd craved as long as she could remember: her own home. Her studio took up the entire basement, and a living room and galley kitchen filled the main floor. Upstairs, her office, bedroom and bathroom made up the rest of the space. She loved it here. She'd renovated the small house, made it her own— her first real private space in the twenty-eight years of her life. Built into the side of a New Hampshire hillside, the back walls were all glass, looking out over a backyard that was more vale than lawn. Here in Mercer she had her home, her art, her friends. This, she thought, is happiness.

"Mason, I live in a tiny house in a tiny town in the middle of nowhere. How much attention could actually find its way all the way to Mercer?"

"Karen," he said softly, "you have no idea."

* * *

Karen hung up the phone after promising to say a prayer for him about the auction, once again wondering what it was about her "face vases" that had such an impact on him.

"Why me, Lacey?" she wondered aloud, thinking back to her first meeting with Mason. The sleeping cat ignored her. "It was like I opened the door and found Indiana Jones standing there."

The comparison with the fictional movie hero wasn't quite accurate, but it wasn't all that far off, either. Mason DuBroc, flamboyant and half-Cajun, with an accent that made folks around Mercer pay attention to every word, definitely took the award for oddest character to ever enter Karen's world. A dubious claim, since a potter's life, by nature of her chosen career, overflowed with artists, collectors and students, most of whom had the usual quirks that went along with a creative spirit. The author of a bestselling book on art crime, Mason had come to Mercer to take up residence at Jackson's Retreat, a writers' colony on the other side of the expansive woods that began almost at Karen's back door.

He'd discovered Karen's vases in the window of a local art gallery, and had immediately sought her out. Mason's fascination with her art intrigued her, but she'd hesitated to ask the larger-than-life character about it, almost as if the interest would evaporate with the inquisition. He thought the vases museum-worthy, and for the past few weeks Mason had been on a mission to raise Karen's profile as an artist. He'd helped her put up a Web site, and he'd sold an article about her to a pottery magazine, which had been reprinted in other publications. The article had led to the *New York Times* publishing two inches of coverage on her last gallery showing in SoHo. Then last week Mason had heard about this auction, and it had quickly become his latest effort.

"I just don't understand, Lord," she whispered. "Why me?"

The front door shot open with a bang, and Karen leaped off the couch with a screech, sending Lacey flying. The cat hit the ground, claws out, and flashed under a chair on the other side of the room as an alto voice rang out over all three floors. "Laurie's daily special was lasagna with peach pie. Hope you're hungry! Are you ever going to start locking that door?"

Karen glared at her best friend as she sailed into the room. "Jane! Are you determined to scare me half to death? What are you doing here?"

Jane Wilson, owner of the Heart's Art Gallery in downtown Mercer, opened her arms in greeting, to-go bag in hand. "Aha! There you are." She held the bag higher. "Lunch! I heard about the vase. Knew you'd need company. Have you talked to Mason about this afternoon's auction?"

Karen blinked. "What?"

"You think he'll be able to buy the vases? He should. I know just his being there will help, but I mean, if he could buy them, you do think he wants to, right? Why wouldn't he? Come on. Lunch is getting cold." Long dark curls swinging around her shoulders, Jane headed for the kitchen.

Karen relented, brushing cat hair from her lap. Jane's enthusiasm flattered her. Jane's gallery anchored Mercer's arts district, and she'd been one of Karen's staunchest supporters since their teens. When Karen had decided ten years ago that she could, in fact, make a living as a potter, Jane had started putting Karen's unique vases and clay art in the windows of her gallery—which was where Mason had first spotted them.

"No idea if he'll be able to buy them or not. I'm still not sure what good this will do."

Jane set the bag on the counter, then turned to pull plates from a cabinet. "Karen, darling, I love your naïveté sometimes. Why don't you make fresh coffee? Your special blend Kona has been on my mind since I left the gallery."

"Jane—"

"No, c'mon, Karen, I'm serious. He's Mason DuBroc. *Dr.* Mason DuBroc. Well-known author of a book on art crime in Middle Eastern war zones so full of adventure that it would make Indiana Jones jealous."

Karen scowled. There was that comparison again. "I *know* who he is, Jane. I knew that when he first showed up on my doorstep."

"Look, girl, Mason may not brag about it around you or around the retreat, but he knows the worth of his own name right now. For him to even bid for your vases—"

"Okay, I get it."

Jane paused in her frenzy of activity. "So what's the problem?"

Karen stood up and walked to the tall windows at the back of the dining area, looking out over the trees that bordered the lawn. Her property sloped down and away from the house, then back up into woods that stretched into the distance.

She loved those woods. There was a path that led

through the heart of them, all the way to the writers' colony where Mason lived. But it had not been the path that had brought him to her door, and she still couldn't shake her confusion about what *had* brought him to her.

Karen cleared her throat. "The problem is that I keep asking, 'Why me?' Why did Mason DuBroc, of all the people on the planet, suddenly focus so much of his interest on my vases and me? What does he want with *me?*"

"Afraid he'll make you successful?"

Karen turned away from the windows. "Don't try to psychoanalyze me, Janie. You're not good at it and I'm not in the mood."

Jane chuckled, a low, throaty sound. "Okay, so you're a little suspicious. I can't blame you. It did seem a little odd when he showed up in the shop, bouncing around the displays and asking all these questions about your vases, but he's an odd bird." She took a deep breath. "Did I tell you that he tried to lecture two of my customers on the relation of your vases to Southern folk art face jugs?" Jane's words picked up speed as she resumed emptying the lunch bag. "I mean, this couple hadn't been in the shop thirty seconds! They fled before I could get out 'Welcome to Mercer, New Hampshire.'"

Karen bit her lip to keep from laughing. "That sounds like him." Joining Jane in the kitchen again, she pulled a bag of Kona coffee from the freezer and a jug of filtered water from her fridge. The sight Mason had made standing on her porch that first day drifted through her mind as she prepared a fresh pot of coffee.

His notoriety intimidated Karen, but his peppered questioning cut to the heart of her craft, its history and its techniques. The accent certainly caught her off guard, as well. Southern but not twangy, the slow, easy-spoken combination of Alabama flatwoods and Louisiana bayou had a thick Cajun edge to it, and when excited, Mason would occasionally season his sentences with French words or phrases that Karen never understood. At least…she thought they were French.

His looks had also gotten her attention, almost as much as the accent. Jane made him sound antic and half-mad, but Mason DuBroc was far from an absentminded professor. His brown eyes were intense and held a curiosity that seemed relentless. His lean frame was wiry, and his dark hair hung mostly straight, with a tendency to curl just on the ends. His eyes and skin were darker than most of the men she knew, and he had high cheekbones so sharp they could have sliced bread. He called himself "a mutt, a result of a lot of familiarity between the Native Americans, Cajuns and a conglomerate of English and Scottish folks hanging out in the Delta," a description that made her own mostly Irish and German heritage sound downright plain.

And the way he smelled. Aromas were vital to Karen, and she didn't know if he wore a cologne or if his scent came naturally from who he was and what he did. He smelled like… Karen searched her mind for a comparison. Like opening a new book in the middle of a pine grove. Maybe a hint of sage. Whatever. It made her want to stand closer to him, and she inhaled deeply, just thinking about it.

"Do you want Parmesan on the lasagna?" Jane asked as she lifted one of the wrapped plates from Laurie's Federal Café. The café was known for its home-style meals and white decor, which Laurie kept scrubbed and polished: solid white tables, chairs and dishes. Laurie refused to use chintzy to-go containers, insisting that the locals were honest enough to return real dishes.

Karen snapped back to the present as the thick garlicky scent of the lasagna got her attention. "What? Oh. Yes."

"Thinking about Mason again?"

Karen sniffed. "No. Yes. A little. Maybe. How is Laurie?"

Jane went with the change of subject as she pulled the wrapped paper off the plates and dusted the Parmesan over the entrées. "Cool as ever. Two of the old farmers who hang out there in the mornings got into some kind of squabble about crop rotation this morning, and she told them she'd start serving only decaf if they didn't quit. Settled them down right away." Jane paused, then picked up the plates and headed to the table. "She also wanted to know if you had turned serious about Mason yet."

Karen pulled two mugs from a cabinet and ignored the question. "How did you hear about the vase?"

Jane barked a laugh. "You've lived here all your life. How do you think I heard?"

"The Peg Madison party line?"

"Her only son may be police chief, but I think she mothers everyone in town. She's worried about you."

Karen watched as the coffeemaker gurgled out its last drops, steam rising from the pot and the filter bucket. Even the scent of the rich, dark coffee refreshed her and she inhaled deeply. "Please tell Mama Peg that I'm fine."

"Which vase was it?"

Karen shrugged. "Too shattered to be sure. One of

the emerald-green ones I made early last year, I think. The bigger shards were green and orange. I did find the mark, but it was just the *KONA,* without the diamond." Every potter scratched a distinctive mark into the bottom of each piece, a way of signing the artwork. At first Karen had used only her initials, *KO,* but over the past two years, her mark had evolved into a distinctive *KONA,* which stood for both her favorite coffee and for Karen *O'Neill Artworks."* Late last year she'd added a diamond shape to it.

She pulled the coffeepot out of the maker and filled the two mugs. "I just don't understand—" She broke off and fanned her free hand as if to wave away the question. "I guess there are nuts in every business."

Jane picked up the plates and headed to the dining table. "Sister, you said a mouthful."

That afternoon, Karen returned to the studio to get her mind off the auction. She soon lost herself in the work. The whirling pot on the wheel before her so captured her that Lacey finally resorted to using claws to get her attention. Karen jumped, an action that caused one finger to break through the wet clay on the wheel, turning a shimmering vase into a pile of mud.

"Lacey!" Karen stopped the wheel, scolding the gray half-Persian at her feet. She cupped the distorted clay mound in both hands while glaring at Lacey. "Look at that!"

The golden eyes of the annoyed feline didn't relent, and the ferocious meow and sharp swish of tail that followed told Karen that she needed to forget about ruined art and open the back door *now.*

"All right!" Karen glanced at a clock near the door and immediately felt a twinge of chagrin. "Four-fifty! No wonder you're desperate." She sighed and headed for the door, followed by the prancing cat. "Sorry about that. I should have let you out before I started. You know how I get."

Meow. Swish.

Karen laughed and used the towel hanging at her waist to open the door to her basement studio. Lacey fled, her thick gray coat a quilt of light and dark shadows as she moved through the fading sunlight. Karen glanced down at the threshold again, but only a light shifting of clay dust remained from this morning. She closed the door again and returned to her wheel, sinking down on the stool behind it, her mouth twisted into a grimace as she gently touched the destroyed vase. It had been on its way to beauty, molded from a brownish lump of clay to an emerald-green work of art. "Sorry."

Karen molded the wet earth back into a ball but didn't restart the wheel, suddenly aware of how tense her shoulders were and how much her back and arms ached. "Four-fifty," she repeated. Almost four hours had passed since she'd sat down at the wheel. Not unusual, though. When the wheel began to turn, the moist clay changing shape beneath her hands, Karen lost track of time, space, even the air around her. Her aunt, Evie, not understanding how Karen could so completely lose herself in the artwork, called it "that thing with the clay." When she worked, Karen's world narrowed to the wheel and the clay, and the only sensations that she remained aware of were the musty smell of damp earth and the feel of the water and earth beneath her hands. She'd been known to work five hours straight as her art formed under her hands. As a result, she usually let Lacey out before she sat down at the wheel, but this afternoon she'd forgotten.

Karen stood, rolling her shoulders, and went to the sink to wash her hands. Time for a break, more coffee, maybe check to see if there were new orders on her fax machine. Or e-mail from Mason. She pulled the towel from the waistband of her jeans and dried her hands.

Karen paused, her hands wrapped in the worn towel, looking at a shelf holding nine vases similar to the ones Mason planned to bid on. Each stood about eighteen inches high, broad at the base, a bit narrower in the middle and flared at the top with the edges jagged and wild, points and curves going in all directions. "Face vases" were not unique in the world of ceramics, but what made Karen's vases distinctive was the face itself. Neither male nor female, it was a horror mask, twisted and grotesque on some, leering and grinning realistically on others. The vase colors were a kaleidoscope nightmare, swirling around the face in stripes and curls. Although each vase featured different colors, the face remained the same, which was especially noticeable when they were lined up together. The same downturned eyes, full lips and white streaks slicked back from the scalp. Of course they're the same, she thought ruefully. They come from the same source.

Tossing the towel over the edge of the sink, Karen headed upstairs, pausing to glance out the windows at the back of the studio at Lacey, now in the process of stalking a wayward butterfly. The metal of the stairs chilled her feet, so she scuffed them a bit on the carpet

of the small dining area that separated the stairs from
the kitchen. She poured the last cup from the lunchtime
pot of Kona into a ceramic mug, and headed up the
stairs near her front door.

A polite scratching on the door stopped her, and she
opened it. "Already?" she asked as Lacey strolled past
her, tail held high. "I thought you were on a butterfly
hunt out back."

No meow this time, just a thank-you figure eight
around Karen's ankles. Then both of them headed
upstairs to Karen's office, where an odd-looking sheet
of paper slowly peeled its way through her fax. She
pulled it off the machine and turned it around.

The fax had rendered it black and white, but the sheet
was clearly a page from an auction house catalog, and
Karen grinned as she recognized the angular, dramatic
handwriting of the phrase scrawled across the bottom.

Lot 21 could be your salvation. Lot 21, which con-
sisted of four unique vases of Karen's own design.

"Sorry, Mason," she murmured, her eyes bright
with amusement. "My salvation comes from a much
higher source."

Yet she knew what he meant, and she glanced at the
Felix the Cat clock on the wall behind her computer:
5:05. The auction must be over by now. The fax machine
clicked and whirred again, and a second sheet emerged.
This one was white, with only four lines scrawled across
it.

$8,000!!! Didn't get them. Will talk to agent who
did. See you tomorrow!! M

The paper fluttered, blurring the words, as her hands
shook. "Eight thousand?" Her knees weakened and

Karen sat hard in her office chair. Tears blurred her eyes. *Two thousand apiece!* She'd never gotten more than five hundred for one of her vases. Mason DuBroc had succeeded in almost quadrupling their value.

Velvety fur brushed her ankles, and Karen glanced down as Lacey circled around her bare feet again. Her hands still quivering, she clicked her tongue and, with a rattling purr and tinkling bell, the eight-pound fur ball landed in her lap. Karen scratched the cat beneath the chin and was rewarded with a swish of Lacey's thick tail.

"Lacey." The shudder in her voice did not surprise her. Karen felt as if she were shivering from head to toe. "I'd better get back to work." She nodded, then reached for the phone. "First I have to call Jane."

Jane insisted on taking Karen to Portsmouth to celebrate, buying her dinner in a cozy boutique restaurant near the water. When they returned, midnight had come and gone, but Karen still felt wired and restless. Wandering into the office, she found fourteen new orders for "face vases" waiting on the fax machine. She glanced through them, overwhelmed. "Oh, Mason. What have we done?"

Sleep helped. The next morning a much calmer Karen awoke early and this time let Lacey out before she even showered. Then she took her first coffee of the day out on the back deck of the house, raising it toward the heavens. "Thank You, Lord," she said aloud. She settled in one of the deck chairs and sipped again, then set the cup on the deck rail and looked out over the yard, feeling blessed. The sun struggled to get above the tallest trees, barely illuminating the May morning with bands of gold shot through the mist. Karen's hair, still darkened from its normal red-gold sheen by her morning shower, dried quickly in the early-morning breeze, and she fluffed it before picking up the mug again.

This was her time. Prayer time. The day never felt quite right without it. The sun now winked at Karen over the top of her tallest birch, and she closed her eyes for a moment. Taking a deep breath, she whispered, "Thank You, Lord. I know Your hand is in all this, all along. Thanks for bringing Mason to Jackson's Retreat to write his book, and thank You for…"

Inside, her phone rang, interrupting her thoughts. She scowled, then looked upward, waiting for the answering machine to pick up. When it did, she returned to her prayer, moving from praise to requests, the last one for herself. "Help me understand all this and Your will in it, Lord."

She sat for a few more moments, enjoying the coffee and the morning air, then headed back inside. She hoped Mason would come by early to talk about the auction, but she had not heard from him since yesterday's fax. Karen left her cup on the bottom step of the staircase, then bounded up, her hair flapping against her neck. Fifteen minutes later, she'd scooted into a pair of jeans and a light sweater, plus her hiking boots in case Mason wanted to walk into Mercer. She'd gone light on the makeup and turned on the blow-dryer long enough that her hair wouldn't completely frizz out as it finished air drying. A touch of mousse, and she was ready just about the time the doorbell rang.

"Coming!" Karen yelled, her boots clumping on the stairs. She kicked over the cup and fussed at herself as she picked it up, thankful it was empty but wishing with a fleeting thought that she had time for another cup of her Kona. She unlocked the front door, pulling it open.

Her cheerful "Good morning!" faded away as she stared at the two men on the front porch. Mason was there, but he looked as solemn as she'd ever seen him. Behind him, oversized hat in hand, stood Tyler Madison, the local police chief.

Mason cleared his throat, but Tyler spoke first. "I hate to bother you this early, Karen, but we've got to talk about your broken vases." He cleared his throat. "Broken vases," he repeated, "and a murder."

TWO

Twice in twenty-four hours, Karen's world flipped upside down. As the two men sat in her living room and laid out their story, she couldn't keep from blurting out, "But who would kill over a vase?"

Luke Knowles, a well-known auction agent, had purchased Lot 21, Karen's vases, bidding the winning $8,000 for an anonymous client. The vases had been delivered to Knowles's hotel room. Late last night, when Luke's wife hadn't been able to reach him, a manager had gone to check, finding Knowles dead and the four vases destroyed.

Karen stared at the two men, a crime scene photo in one hand and empty coffee cup in her other. "Who?" she repeated.

Tyler and Mason shifted uncomfortably and glanced at each other, then Mason touched her arm gently. "We were hoping you could help with that."

Blinking, Karen looked down at the photo in her hand again, the details registering sketchily on her mind. A hotel room in chaos; in the center, ceramic shards and clay dust—remnants of four destroyed vases—were smeared across a dresser. At the edge of the image, a man's leg protruded into the scene. The victim, murdered because of vases she had created from her imagination and a bit of raw clay.

The photo quivered as her fingers trembled, and Karen sat hard on her sofa. Her pottery, her art, was her heart, her livelihood and her life. Her vases, beautiful and distinct, sometimes felt like extensions of her very soul.

But they weren't worth dying over.

Karen stared into her empty coffee cup as the two men sat and Tyler finished telling her about the death of Luke Knowles. She relished the security of the hard, cool ceramic under her fingertips as her eyelids stung and her vision blurred. Tyler sat across from her, his bulky frame wedged into one of her grandmother's ancient, cane-bottom rockers, his hat clutched in one fist and a file folder in the other. Mason perched next to her on the edge of her fading rose-print sofa, his jeans a stark contrast to the feminine blossoms splayed under his thighs.

The morning sun had broken free of the tall trees of her backyard and now cast bright yellow streaks through the windows. The room seemed to glow, despite the somber mood of the three people clustered there.

"What about his family?" Karen's voice was a strained whisper. "Did he have a family?" She peered at Mason, then Tyler. Her stomach felt tight, her chest constricted, but she wasn't sure if she felt fear or grief. Or both. Hot tears leaked from each eye, and she wiped them away quickly.

The young police chief nodded. "A wife and a grown son."

"I don't understand." Her soft voice cracked, and

she swallowed again. "Why would anyone do this because of me?"

Tyler shifted in the chair, causing the cane to creak ominously. "Just like there was a note with your broken vases, there was a note at the crime scene." He pulled a slip of paper from a file folder and held it out toward her. Mason stood quickly and helped the paper make the cross to Karen. He slipped the photo from her fingers and returned it to Tyler.

"That's a copy they faxed," Tyler explained. "The detective in New York thought you might recognize the handwriting."

Karen wiped her eyes again and sat the cup on the floor near her feet. She unfolded the note, her fingers trembling a bit. As if scrawled and smeared with a pen too large for the writer's hand, the letters swirled in an almost unreadable script in the middle of the page. She studied the note, her shoulders bowing slightly as a tight chill settled at the base of her spine. She recognized the handwriting...but not from anyone she knew. The clumsy block letters were the same as in the notes that had simply said, Stop! This one, however, was more specific.

Evil corrupts mind and soul.
Evil must be stopped.
All that is evil will be destroyed.

Her head snapped toward Mason, then Tyler. "So the killer thinks my vases are evil? Or me?"

Tyler shrugged. "New York thinks it could go either way. He could be a nutcase who has a fixation on your work, or maybe he has a problem with you personally. Or it could be a jealous—"

"But...*evil?*"

Mason cleared his throat. "Work or personal, this is about you."

Tyler shifted in the rocker, his mouth pursed around a word that never made it out.

"But why?" Karen stood up and took the cup into the kitchen. Tyler caught the note as she passed by, slipping it from her fingers and returning it to the folder. She continued into the kitchen, her energy surging. She set the cup down with a solid thump on the counter that divided the two rooms. "They're just vases." She tapped her temple. "They just came out of my imagination and whatever I've learned about pots through the years." She held her hand out toward Mason. "You know that. We talked about this!"

"I know." He followed her into the kitchen. "But you're trying to make sense of something that may exist only in this guy's head. He killed because of something that makes sense only to him."

Karen grabbed a dishcloth off the sink and began to wipe off an already spotless counter. "But if he thinks the vases are evil, then he thinks *I'm* evil."

"Which is why we're here."

"Because evil must be destroyed."

Tyler's gaze bounced between the two, and he finally intervened. "Well, it's clear neither of you is a cop." He joined them at the counter. "Calm down." He perched on one of the three bar stools that stood guard on the living room side of the counter. "First of all, New York does not expect you to figure out what's going on with this murderer. That's their job. Second, no one really thinks *you* are in danger. If whoever this is wanted to hurt *you…*" Tyler paused and shifted on the stool. "After all, he's already proven he knows where you live."

"But—"

"Which is why she needs protection!"

Tyler held up his hand to both of them. "And this is a small town. Everyone around knows the first thing you do every morning is make a pot of that fancy Hawaiian coffee you have shipped in and go out on your deck to talk to God. If the killer wanted you, he wouldn't be wasting time and money buying up vases to shoot. Even a perfect stranger could sit at Laurie's café for a couple of days and figure out what your schedule is." Tyler shook his head. "We'll add extra drive-bys on patrol, but the truth is, even a 24/7 guard probably wouldn't help. Whatever his problem is, he wants to get rid of the vases, not you."

Karen felt the heat slowly rise from her throat to her cheeks. "Every one?"

Tyler grinned. "My mom thinks it's cute that you have a different robe for every season." He stood, his mood somber again. "I do want you to take extra pre-cautions. Make sure you lock the doors and set the alarm. Don't wander around alone too much. And call me if you see anything strange—" he looked down at Lacey, who had suddenly started climbing his pants leg "—other than this cat—about the house." He plucked Lacey off and put her on the stool. "In the meantime, I think you two should go for breakfast."

Karen's eyes widened. *Food?* "You don't think I can eat now, do you?"

Tyler wandered toward the door, his eyes glancing casually around the room. "I certainly think you *should* eat. Mason has agreed to talk to you about the vases, see if you remember anything unusual about them. Maybe something about those particular vases strikes a chord with you."

"But—"

"Protein. Eat some meat. Eggs. Lots of water." He tapped the side of his head as he reached for the doorknob. "Helps you think."

Mason followed him, an almost bemused smile on his face, and Karen wondered if the Delta boy thought their local police chief to be a dolt—or small-town clever. She walked out onto the deck again, staring, embracing the way the remaining mist seeped into her bones, as if the sting of it reminded her that she was still among the living.

"Lord," she whispered, "what's going on?"

Mason held the door for Tyler, who paused, glancing around him at Karen. Although Mason stood an inch or two taller than the young police chief, he admired the almost graceful way Tyler moved his larger, more muscular frame. Definitely not a man he'd want to oppose in a fight.

Tyler's voice dropped in tone as well as volume. "You watch out for her. I knew she'd take it hard, but not this hard."

Mason nodded. "She has a gentle soul." A soul he had a sudden urge to protect.

Tyler's eyes brightened a moment but he said nothing, and Mason twisted a bit under the police chief's gaze. "You really don't think she's in danger? This has already escalated from broken vases to murder. That's quite a leap!"

Tyler straightened. "I meant what I said to her. But let's not forget something. Luke Knowles died because this guy wanted to be taken seriously—and not just as a crackpot who likes breaking pottery. He wants those vases to go away." Tyler shifted his weight. "Karen may not be in danger right now, but that doesn't mean this won't escalate even more. We'll do what we can, but watch your back. And hers."

Mason watched, thoughtful as Tyler's patrol car backed away, tires crunching on the narrow gravel drive. On the way over, Tyler had explained that since no threat had been made against Karen, he was limited in how much action he could take to protect her. He could add the extra drive-bys, but with only a five-officer force, no one could be there 24/7.

Inside again, Mason shut the door and turned, his eyes focusing on Karen's back. Her shoulders slumped forward as she leaned heavily against the deck railing, and Mason wondered if she were praying again. She did that a lot, more than he was used to his friends doing, and it created an odd ache just below his sternum that he couldn't quite explain. It wasn't that he didn't believe; he'd accepted Christ as his Savior fifteen years ago, at a youth rally when he was nineteen. His faith, however, was a closely held, private thing. Few of his friends even knew he was a Christian, and he was comfortable with that. He didn't want to discuss his faith, definitely didn't want to discuss theirs. His chosen profession, and his public image, didn't lend themselves to outward shows of belief. Yet the highly visible nature of Karen's faith left him with a nagging urge to ask questions.

And her faith was not the only thing that tugged at him, almost without explanation. From the moment he'd seen her vases in Jane's shop, his imagination had been captured by her talent, her sense of color and shape, by how the vases seemed almost organic, as if they had been grown instead of formed from clay. Then, when she'd opened the door that day, covered in mud up to her elbows, hair wild and her eyes dazed, as if he'd interrupted a dream…

Mason rubbed his mouth. He didn't like that he could not find the right words to the feelings that tightened his chest and made his mind whirl whenever he was around her…troublesome, since words were his business. He didn't like it at all.

He did, however, like her. Maybe even more than *like.* He shifted his weight from one foot to the other. Being around Karen felt like…home. Mason had never quite believed that God had a chosen path for everyone, and that He could guide each person to it. Yet he'd been planning to go to a retreat center in Georgia when he got the call about the opening at Jackson's Retreat. He'd never been to New Hampshire. The day he saw her vases in Jane's window he had planned to stay in Boston, but his appointment had been canceled.

True, he could explain all that away, but not the way his heart had jumped when she'd opened the door. The way he longed to stand close to her, protect her. He tried desperately not to crowd or smother her; he'd already seen how carefully she kept people at a distance. Her aunt. Even Jane.

"Lord," he muttered. "If this is Your path for us, You have a lot of work to do."

Mason opened the door to the deck and approached Karen quietly, waiting until she raised her head again and turned toward him. Her eyes glistened, and she licked tears off her lower lip.

His heart twisted. "Praying for Luke Knowles?"

She wiped her eyes, smearing her mascara. "And his family. And for guidance."

"Guidance?"

She nodded. "I suspect we're going to need all the help we can get."

"We?"

Karen's eyebrows arched. "You don't think we're going to sit here and do nothing?"

A grin slowly crossed his face. "You? I can't see you sitting still for much of anything."

She waved a hand and marched past him. "Then come with me."

Mason's curiosity took over. "Where are you going?"

She kept walking, but pointed at the floor. "Down." She headed for the far corner of her living room, away from the kitchen, where an elegant spiral staircase circled down to her pottery studio. Since he usually entered the studio from the outside, he took each of the narrow steps carefully, especially avoiding the coffee cup she'd left on a step about halfway down. The custom-built steps were barely deep enough for his size tens, and he arrived at the bottom long after Karen had disappeared from view.

Mason paused, looking around. The studio, which took up the entire basement, was Karen's sanctuary, and she kept it pristinely clean. The house was set deep into a solid granite hillside, and three walls of the basement had been framed directly against the stone, which still protruded through the Sheetrock in places. Shelves lined almost every inch, clustered with baskets of paints, clays, glazes, molds, texturing tools and the round, flat bats for the three potter's wheels that stood in a line in the center of the room. Every shelf was labeled and each basket neatly organized. At one end of the room stood an extruding table, where Karen pulled thin plates of clay for hand building. Next to the table stood a work-table stained with years of glaze, paint and old bits of clay. At the other end sat two kilns, one for her larger projects and one that wasn't much bigger than a toaster oven, in which she made the smaller gifts and beads for local jewelry artists. The glass wall that overlooked the hill was spotless and dotted with sun catchers.

The potter, however, could not be seen. "Where are you?"

"Back here." Her head seemed to appear suddenly out of a space of granite. Puzzled, Mason crossed the room to discover that there was a thin doorway in the rock, disguised by the gray stone directly behind it and revealed only by a yellow light now coming from the left.

Karen stepped out.

"A baffle?"

She nodded. "When the house was built, the owner wanted a darkroom, and the builder tried to carve this Z in the rock as a rough sort of light baffle. Rumor has it that it drove two of his workers completely crazy. Unfortunately, it was all for naught. The owner died before the house was complete. I like it." She grinned. "When

the light's off, you can't even tell there's a room here."
She stepped back and Mason trailed her around the tight
corner of the thin, Z-shaped baffle into a room of granite
walls with high shelves along one side.

He looked up and around, his eyes widening. "This
is amazing! Like a catacomb." The cavelike room was
barely four feet wide and extended back into the stone
about eight feet. A bare bulb hung from a hook driven
into the stone ceiling, small, but casting enough light
that he could read the labels on the neat, clearly marked
metal boxes that covered the shelves.

Karen's smile broadened. "My secret hiding place."
She turned suddenly and pulled a file box from one of
the middle shelves. "But this is what I came for."

He took it from her, and a slightly surprised look
crossed her face. "What's wrong, *chère?*" he asked.

She blinked. "Guess I'm not used to having anyone
help me." She shrugged, then motioned for him to leave.
"Let's take it back out there."

They exited the room, and she snapped off the light
behind them, letting her private storage room disappear
into the wall again. He set the box on her worktable and
she flipped the lid up and back, letting it bang against
the tabletop. Inside were stacks of small, five-by-seven
photo albums. "That was the Wilhelms auction, right?"

When he nodded, her lips pursed. "The four in that
catalog were old, earlier versions. I stopped using
orange last year, went solely to streaks of green and
red…and I don't remember selling to a Wil…" Her
voice faded a moment as her eyes closed. "A set of four.
Not a private sale, must have been through one of the
galleries. Haven't sold four at once except…" another

pause, then her eyes flew open and she attacked the box, digging through the albums "…2005. A dealer, but not in New York. Boston. Told me he'd sold four as a gift. A woman was giving them to her mother. She bargained him down to about a hundred dollars per."

"She got a good deal."

Karen clutched a red binder and pulled it out, plopping it down on the table. She opened it, pausing briefly at the first page, her fingers resting lightly on the first picture.

Mason peered at the yellowed photo. "What is it?"

Her childlike smile reminded him of a young girl caught in an embarrassing moment. "I'd forgotten this was here. These are the first four vases I sold."

Mason gently pulled her hand back to reveal a shot of four vases in deep blues and vibrant emerald greens. No faces, yet the elegance of their simple lines enchanted the eye. "They're beautiful."

She sighed. "I adored them. Almost wish I had them back, but if I hadn't sold them, I wouldn't have known I could do this for a living. They were my breakthrough pieces."

"Who bought them?"

"A dealer on New York's Lower East Side." She looked at the far wall of the studio, thoughtful, her gaze distant. "Tiny place. Brand-new. We were both trying to give each other a hand up. He bought them for thirty-five dollars, sold them for fifty dollars."

Karen sighed as if she were savoring a favorite memory, and Mason touched her hand. "Do you know who purchased them from the dealer?"

She turned to him, her smile sad. "No. I wish I did.

It would be like finding out what had happened to an old fri—" Her words faded, and as they continued to look at each other a few moments, Mason felt as if whatever it was between them had gently escalated. Mason felt her tremble, and the urge to kiss her, to hold her, washed over him. He leaned forward, his lips close to hers, but Karen suddenly tensed.

Karen cleared her throat and looked away, turning the album page quickly.

Heat shot into Mason's cheeks and he released her hand. "*Chère,* I'm sorry."

Karen stared at the photos. "No, don't be. I mean…it's okay. I just…" She glanced quickly at him, then back at the table. "Not the right time, with Luke Knowles and all." She patted the photos. "We need to do this." She faced him again, worry clouding her eyes. "Right?"

You idiot! Mason scolded himself. To Karen, he nodded. "Of course. You're right." He squared his shoulders and let out a deep breath. "In fact, we wouldn't even have to do this if I hadn't been a dolt and left the catalog in New York. Show me what you have."

She then flipped several more pages, and Mason watched as the shots passed—pages of pots, plaques, vases, teapots, wall sculptures that flashed by under her fingers.

"You keep pictures of *everything?*"

"Yep. Polaroids of the older ones. Now I use digital shots, keep them on CDs. Helps me track ideas, sales, if I want to duplicate, or if I want to *avoid* duplicating…" She stopped and flattened her hand over one page. She took a deep breath, then pushed the album toward him. "Here they are."

He peered at the picture, which had yellowed a bit with age, remembering the page from the auction catalog. There they were, indeed, identical, the swirling colors and the faces with the dark hair with white streaks distinctive even in this small photo. His bidding duel with Luke Knowles flashed through his head, and Mason swallowed. "They're remarkable." He didn't want to think about what might have happened had he succeeded in buying the vases. Or if the killer decided to turn his sights on Karen. His throat tightened, making his voice more guttural than he'd expected.

She shook her head. "But not worth killing for." Karen glanced at the picture, then focused on him, her hand closing on his wrist. "What's the matter?"

Mason's hand seemed to tingle from her touch, and he felt heat rising in his cheeks. Her eyes were so *blue*. Almost cobalt, like the Atlantic in the high sun. But he wouldn't approach her again. Not today. He cleared his throat. "We should probably take a copy of this to Tyler."

Those blue eyes gleamed. "Of course. But that's not what's wrong."

There was no way…no…he would *not* talk about… One embarrassing moment a day was quite enough.

Karen broke the moment, pulling away and slipping the photo out of the album. She pointed to the address on the back. "That's the dealer who bought them." She paused, looking over him again. "Maybe Tyler was right. Breakfast might be a good idea after all. We could stop on the way to Tyler's office."

"Yes," Mason said quickly. "Some of Laurie's French toast might just do the trick."

Karen grinned, then headed back toward the stairs, grabbing her cup as she went. "Absolutely."

Mason followed her up the twisting steps, pausing briefly at the top. The sun, now slowly heating the living room to a comfortable toast, streaked her hair with gold, and the curls bounced as she walked to the kitchen, making him smile. She set the cup down, then pulled an envelope out of a drawer and slid the picture in. She flipped off the coffeemaker and grabbed her purse from a stool near the bar. "Did you drive?"

He shook his head. "Tyler drove us over from his office."

"Let's walk then. Work off a few of Laurie's calories before we eat them— What?"

Mason hesitated. He didn't want to say it, but all the girls he'd known would have killed him if he'd held back, especially with them going out. He reached out and touched her cheek, just below her left eye. "Your mascara…the tears…"

Her cheeks reddened, but her smile was one of delight. "You doll," she said. "Thank you." She bounded up the stairs, to return only a minute or so later, her face clean and eyelashes darkened again. "Better?"

He nodded, and she paused to set the alarm before shooing him toward the door. She locked it behind them, her key slipping easily in and out of the dead bolt. "By the way, how did you hook up with Tyler this morning?"

"The police contacted me in New York, after Luke Knowles was shot. They had asked the auction house about other bidders, and the auctioneer gave them my name. They said they'd leave contacting you up to the local cop, Tyler, and I called him, asking if I could come with him."

Karen nodded. "Why did you want to come?"

He hesitated. "To be here for you. I thought you might take it pretty hard."

She considered this a moment, then he barely heard her quiet "Thank you."

The hillside cottage was three blocks downhill from the center of town, and as they plodded upward, Mason was glad there was still a slight chill in the morning air. They fell silent for a few moments, the only sound the solid padding of their hiking boots on the rough pavement. Mason shortened his strides to match hers, feeling far too much like a lanky colt next to her elegance. Karen barely came up to his shoulder, but she had a toned, athletic build and she moved with a smooth grace. Occasionally, she'd get focused or forgetful and experience a sudden klutziness, which charmed him even more.

Yet Mason's enjoyment of Mercer, New Hampshire, extended far beyond the climate and Karen's friendship. The tight-knit community, with its Revolutionary War history and art district ambience had totally charmed him. Most of the families had been in the area for almost three hundred years, with the exception of a cluster of artists who'd started flocking to the town in the late sixties.

Their presence had given rise to an active local arts society, a number of unique galleries and the writers' colony, where he lived. There was a lot of encouragement for homegrown artists, including the one who now strolled at his side while he struggled not to stare.

Karen walked with her head up as they moved along the narrow lane toward Mercer's main street. Her gaze darted along the scenery, as if recording and storing every detail of the morning. She paused occasionally to give an extra second to a squirrel, an unusual red flower or an odd shadow in the trees. After she'd stopped to finger a leaf left over from last fall, one turned to a lacey fringe by bugs and frost, Mason finally gave in to his curiosity. "What do you see in that?"

She held it in her palm, smoothing a bit of mud off the stem. "The pattern. I've been making some 'nature' trays for one of the galleries. Hand-built. I press plants, berries, grasses, that kind of thing, into the clay to create the pattern. When it's fired, the foliage burns off but leaves the pattern. I paint the illustrations in and around the impressions."

He stopped at the crossroad at the end of her street to check traffic, then took her elbow as they turned toward town again. "Is that what you did with the vases?"

Silent, Karen stared down at the leaf, lying feather-like in her hand.

Mason pulled her to a halt. "Karen?"

She continued to look down. "If I tell you this, you can't ever, ever put it in writing. You promise?"

Mason reached for her chin and pulled her head up. "I promise."

"I don't want anyone to think I'm crazy." Her gaze grew even more distant. "My aunt already thinks…" Her words faded.

He dropped his hand to her shoulder, tilting his head to look more closely at her. "Karen, you are one of the least crazy people I know. So tell me."

She licked her lips. "Those vases…they've evolved. I kinda do my own thing now, trying to keep them new."

"But?"

She finally met his eyes. "But the first ones came to me in a dream several years ago."

Okay, so she *could* surprise him. "A dream?"

She sighed. "A nightmare, actually." She pulled the envelope from her purse and slipped the leaf in as she pulled the photo out. She ran her finger over the image. "Several of them. This face." Her eyelids lowered, shadowing her gaze. "It was not long after the first show at that little gallery on East Houston. Small, but I got good notices. Sold those pieces I showed you, and it looked as if I could truly do this for a living."

Karen took a deep breath and opened her eyes, looking directly into his. "A couple of weeks later, I started having nightmares about being chased. I couldn't tell who it was, but there was this face." She tapped the photo again. "*This* face. So pale, with the white streaks in dark hair. The sharp nose, high cheekbones. And legs. Thick, running legs. Green legs. I woke up in such a panic that I …" She swallowed. "I'd never felt a fear like that. I did the first vase in an attempt to get rid of the nightmare. I never expected to sell it—or that it would be the start of dozens of others."

"What about the nightmare?"

"It disappeared." Karen returned the photo to the envelope and put it back in her purse. "I've always been able to work out things like that in the art. It's as if all I have to do is to get it out of my head and into the clay, then things work out."

"Any idea what the dream meant?"

She frowned. "You mean, like an interpretation?"

"Sure. It's not as New Agey as it sounds." He took a deep breath, remembering something he'd heard not long after becoming a Christian. "After all, the Bible is full of dreams and visions, and most meant something significant." He took her hand. "There are a number of books out there…some people think dreams are one way God answers prayers."

Karen stared at him a few minutes, then raised her head a bit. "I'll have to think about that one." She nodded. "And I know just who to talk to." Grinning, she slipped her hand out of his and took his arm as they resumed walking. "In the meantime, let's get some French toast."

The warmth of her hand against his skin made Mason stand a little taller as they entered downtown Mercer. Laurie's Federal Café occupied a tiny storefront about halfway between the granite city hall at one end of town and the millpond at the other. Her two "mission statements" hung near the register: Good Food Served Simply and We Trust In God; All Others Must Pay Cash.

The lanky blonde with a red face waved at Mason and Karen from the back counter of the restaurant as they helped themselves to seats near the door. Karen barely had time to drape her purse on the back of her chair before Laurie was at their side with a coffeepot and two cups. She touched Karen's shoulder as she filled the mugs. "Just plain old coffee, but fresh and hot. Tell me you're having French toast."

Mason took a long sniff of the coffee, and his smile grew lazy and broad. "You know it, pretty lady. Your French toast makes life a little better."

Laurie looked down at him, her eyes bright and flirtatious. "You need to bring your older brothers up here, if they talk like you." As the heat rose in his cheeks, she laughed. "And especially if they blush like you."

"French toast is not protein."

Mason twisted in his seat at the sound of Tyler's baritone voice to find the officer standing behind him. "No," he agreed, "but it's some mighty fine eating."

"Following us, Mr. Madison?" Karen's voice teased, but she pulled out the extra chair at the table and motioned for him to sit.

He did, removing his hat. "Not yet. We're out of coffee at the station, so I came over to get some to-go cups. Mom won't go to the grocery until this afternoon."

"Mom?" Mason asked.

Tyler cleared his throat. "My mother is office manager for the police department."

"Peg's terrific," Karen said. "She's like a mom to the whole town."

Tyler shifted in his chair, then focused on Karen. "How are you doing?"

She examined her fingernails. "I'm all right. I think."

Mason touched her arm. "Show him the picture."

Karen perked back to life. "Oh!" She dug in her purse, pulling out the envelope and handing Tyler the Polaroid. "Those are the four vases. I sold them originally to a dealer in Boston. The name is on the back of the photo, but they moved recently. I'll e-mail you the new address."

"Please do. You never know where a clue may pop up." He held the photo close to his face, studying every detail. "Are they distinctive?"

She shook her head. "Not exactly. I do a lot of vases, many of them of a similar design. Each vase is unique, unlike the others in some way, but they are all of the same type."

Tyler rubbed his thumb over the print. "What's this face on them?"

Karen shot a warning glance at Mason and shook her head. "Just one of my trademarks. I do a lot of face vases. They're my bestselling item."

"Is it always the same face?"

"More or less. As I said, my trademark. It's what people expect on a Karen O'Neill face vase."

"That's what drew me to do the article," Mason interjected.

Tyler looked up at him. "What article?"

Mason explained about the magazine article he'd written and his own interest in "face vases." "One of my grandmothers had a couple of 'face jugs,' which tend to be prominent in the South. But sculpting face masks on pottery artifacts is centuries old. Usually they're stylized, even exaggerated or grotesque."

Tyler peered at the picture again. "So this isn't anyone in particular?"

Karen shook her head. "No. Like I said, it's just out of my head."

The young police chief squinted. "Looks familiar, though. Are you sure this isn't based on someone you know?"

Karen's curls trembled and her lips tightened. "Positive."

Mason watched, his brow tensing. "It's the same with writers."

Tyler looked up from the picture, puzzled by the interruption. "Beg pardon?"

Mason spoke quickly. "Novelists, I mean. They don't usually base a character on any one specific person. Too easy to get sued, especially nowadays. Characters tend to be composites of people they know, folks they think they know and stuff they just make up. Artists do the same sometimes, especially with abstractions or art like this. Not real. A representation of real."

"Ah." Tyler looked back at the photo, obviously not completely convinced. "Good job making it look familiar, anyway. Do you mind if I take this? I'll get it scanned and get it back to you within a couple of days. And don't forget to e-mail me that address. I'm sure New York would like to know how the vases got to that auction."

Karen sighed, a touch of relief on her face. "Keep it as long as you need it. But would you e-mail me the scan? I've been meaning to get that done to the old pictures anyway."

Tyler tucked the picture into his shirt pocket as Laurie brought his four coffees to go in a cardboard box. "Sure. I'll send it over as soon as I have it." He stood, put his hat on, then handed Laurie a five-dollar bill as he took the box. "Thanks."

Mason watched him go, then turned to find Karen staring at him. "What?" he asked.

"You didn't have to do that."

He glanced up at Laurie as she set his plate in front of him. "Thanks, Miss Laurie," he said, picking up his knife and fork. "It looks better than anything even my mama ever put in front of me."

Laurie grinned. "Thanks, sugar," she said, picking up

on his accent. She placed Karen's plate down and winked at her. "Don't let him sweet-talk you into anything."

Karen stifled a giggle. "I won't."

Mason looked from one to the other, his eyes carefully held wide in what he hoped was an expression of innocence. "I have no idea what y'all are talking about."

"Oh, I'm sure you don't." Laurie refilled their cups and beat a discreet retreat.

Mason watched her for a second, then turned back to Karen. "I didn't have to do what?" he asked, a bite of French toast crowding one cheek.

"Distract Tyler. Thank you for doing it. That was just weird, him looking at the vase as if it were someone he knew."

Mason swallowed and looked her over carefully. "Karen, how long has Tyler been a cop?"

She paused. "Not sure. Since college, I know. We went to high school together, but he's older and I didn't really pay attention. Maybe ten years. Why?"

"All that time here?"

"Yeah, I guess."

He leaned back in his chair. "I know how you feel about the vases and that face, but you need to think about something, as well. Tyler's powers of observation are skilled. Trained. This is a small town. He's going to know most people in this area. Has to—it's his job. Cops I knew back home could tell you family histories for every kid at the local high school, including who their granddaddies ran around with when they were kids. If he thinks he recognizes the face, then he probably does."

Karen stared at her plate. "I don't want to hear this."

"Why? What if he's right? What if your memory is picking up on someone you really know and plopping it on those vases?"

She put down her fork and turned to him. "It can't be."

"Why not?"

She took a deep breath and dropped her voice so low that he had to lean forward to hear her. "Don't you understand? That face was *chasing* me. I was running away because I was terrified. I was running because the person attached to that face was trying to kill me." Karen leaned back, watching Mason closely, waiting for a response.

He took a deep breath, not wanting to say the words that begged to come out. But if her dreams were a memory trying to work its way out, they were the logical response, the only response. He swallowed hard, dropping his voice. "So has anyone ever really tried to kill you?"

Karen's eyes met his, evenly, solidly. "Yes."

From a car across the street, the cold eyes of Luke Knowles's client watched Karen and Mason's intimate conversation. "How cozy. Whispering sweetness to him?" The soft voice spoke in the smooth cadences of a practiced speaker, despite the New England edge it held.

The client had not expected Karen and Mason to leave the house so soon, but this provided an advantage, opening up the time frame for the plan by at least fifteen minutes. The client chuckled. A lot could be accomplished in fifteen minutes.

Those blue eyes finally looked away from the café, scanning the street, the mostly closed storefronts. Watching carefully each movement, each blown leaf or strolling citizen. Despicable little town, actually, with its pretentious quaintness and that laughable "arts district." When this was all over, leaving would be a pleasure as well as a necessity.

But not yet. There was still much to be done, although the first parts of the plan were already in play. First Knowles, now…

The client watched as Tyler Madison bounded out of his office and ran up the street toward the arts district, more lumbering bull than sprinting elk. Even from this distance, the client could hear the rattle and squeak of the leather and metal belts and instruments hanging from the police chief's body. An even younger—and substantially thinner—officer soon followed, and the client smiled and sat straighter, starting the car's engine and slipping the car away from the curb. Time for the next step.

THREE

Karen watched as Mason froze for a second, then struggled to swallow the remaining bit of French toast. "You're not joking, are you?" His voice had a note of disbelief in it, almost as if he wanted her to say she'd only been kidding. He took a quick gulp of coffee, then cleared his throat. "Is this about your parents?"

Karen closed her eyes. She didn't want to think about it, much less talk about it, but it wasn't as if it was a big secret; everyone who'd been in Mercer more than a few years knew. She should have realized he would have heard about her parents by now, if not all the details where she was concerned. Sooner or later, Tyler would bring it up, anyway…better that Mason not be caught off guard.

She pushed her plate away and leaned toward him. "Yes. My parents were murdered. I don't know what you've heard, but when I was seven…" Her voice trailed off. No, that was not the way to tell him. She took a deep breath and sat a little straighter, waving away the previous words with one hand. "Most of what I know I've learned from folks around town. Old newspapers." She sighed. "My aunt won't talk about—but other people have said—" *Why is this so hard to say to him!* "My father," she said slowly, "was a real estate agent, one of the most successful in the area. Mom stayed at home with me, and she wanted to make sure neither of us ever got bored. She enrolled me in all kinds of stuff—dance classes, art camps, community theater. I've been told she was sweet but quite the determined stage mom. I think she might have had designs on me being a star someday."

Mason remained still, silent; his eyes focused solely on her face. He did nothing to confirm what he had heard…or what he hadn't. He just listened.

She took a sip of the coffee. "That day, they tell me I tried out for a local production of *Annie*. The director later told the police that they loved me. Gave me the role on the spot. My aunt says I had a voice that could make the rafters shake. Mom was so proud. Later, the cops assumed that instead of going home, we went to find Daddy to tell him, to celebrate. Mom had called his office, and his assistant told her about one of his open houses, gave her the address."

She stopped, hitting the wall of darkness that always occurred at this point in the story. She looked down at her fingernails. Sometimes she wanted to remember; mostly she was glad she couldn't. Everyone who knew—and sometimes that felt like the whole town— said it was for the best that she never recalled what happened next. Karen took a deep breath.

"Sometime after we arrived, my parents were attacked and killed. Stabbed. A neighbor heard my mother screaming and called the police, but my parents were dead by the time they arrived. They found me in the backyard, bloody and catatonic but alive."

Mason, frozen in place, muttered something under his breath that she couldn't quite hear. From the dark look on his face, she was afraid to ask.

"The next thing I remember," she finished up, "is seeing my uncle Jake when I woke up in the hospital." She reached for the coffee again. "He had to tell me my parents were gone. No one else would."

Mason waited, but Karen couldn't say anything more. She closed her fingers around the cup and tightened her lips, trying to hold back the tears that, more than twenty years after the murders, still edged in from the corners of her eyes.

Finally he let out a long breath. "Is Jake the one who raised you?"

Karen stared at him. Even though the whole town knew the basics of the most infamous unsolved murder in the area, no one who asked about it focused on what had happened afterward. She'd heard enough gasps of shock to last a lifetime. Questions about the killer, whom she couldn't remember, still swirled in her head. Folks had patted her arm and politely offered their condolences, even years later.

No one had ever asked about the aftermath for her.

She studied him. "Why did you ask that?"

His eyebrows shot up. "I guess it's the next logical question. The person who came to you in the hospital should be next of kin. I mean, you've mentioned that he was your mentor with the pottery, but I don't think I realized how far back your relationship went."

She frowned, unsure of his line of thinking. "Jake wasn't my uncle at the time. Now he is."

It was Mason's turn to look confused. He lowered

his head and peered at her through his eyelashes. "Say that again."

Shaking her head, Karen suppressed a grin. "Jake is my uncle now because he married my aunt. Back then, they were still dating." Her mouth twisted. "My family was odd during that time. Aunt Evie wasn't sure she wanted to marry an artist, but Jake eventually persuaded her. Shane, my cousin, had it pretty rough, especially before Jake came along. Despite the family money, I've heard that my grandmother Elizabeth hated him, made him work for every reward. Jake helped smooth the tension in the family, but Shane left as soon as he could, joined the army and got out. He's in real estate now. Aunt Evie married pretty young the first time, but her first husband never came back from Vietnam. I guess that's a bit complex."

"Not if you're from the South," he muttered. "So Jake did wind up raising you?"

"And teaching me pottery—"

"Can you two come with me?"

Karen jumped, twisting to stare at Tyler, who stood behind her chair. Neither of them had heard him come in.

"Now?" Mason asked.

The solemn look didn't leave Tyler's face. "Now. Right now."

Karen glanced at Mason, but he didn't hesitate. He stood, dropped a twenty on the table and waved his thanks at Laurie. They followed Tyler onto the sidewalk, where he paused only briefly, turning them north toward the tiny arts district of Mercer, speaking as he picked up speed. "Someone broke in to Jane's gallery and destroyed every piece you had on display."

* * *

Jane Wilson's Heart's Art Gallery stood on the corner of Main Street and Fourth, the best location possible, just at the entrance to the Fourth Street Arts Arcade. The rapid growth of Mercer's arts community in the seventies and eighties had led to an accompanying expansion of tourists to downtown, especially in the summer. The town council had designated Fourth Street as a pedestrian area, closing three blocks of it to motor traffic and planting trees down the middle. Jane's gallery, specializing in folk art of the area, had flourished, and she'd become one of Karen's main vendors—and a close friend.

The corner location meant windows on two sides of the shop, giving ample display and natural light for her wares. Now, one of those windows lay shattered in the street, and Jane was visible through the broken pane, shuddering as she hugged herself. Seeing her from half a block away, Karen called her name and ran to her, engulfing her in a hug as Jane collapsed against her. Her friend's tears soaked her shirt, and Karen stroked her back. "What happened?"

"I don't know," Jane said, her voice clogged. "It was like this when I came to open this morning."

Karen heard Mason and Tyler approach from behind. "What was taken?" Mason asked.

Jane's head snapped up. "Nothing!" She motioned wildly at the gallery. "They did all this and took nothing! All they did was break the window and Karen's pieces. I can understand stealing them, but to just destroy them?" Jane's voice bordered on hysterical. "It makes no sense!"

Mason looked from the window to Tyler. "Did you find another note?"

Karen stared at him, startled that his mind would go

toward the investigation so quickly, then at Tyler, who said flatly, "Yes. Same message. I bagged it for the lab in New York."

Jane stepped back, looking at all of them. "How did you know?"

Mason moved closer to Tyler. "Why was the window broken from the inside? Just maliciousness?"

Tyler shook his head, then squatted next to the broken glass, pulling a pen from his pocket. Mason joined him as the police chief moved two of the shards slightly, pushing them closer together. "It was shot from inside, here. We found the bullet in the wall across the street. But the bullet wasn't just to shatter the glass. The shot was to make a point." He made a circling motion with the pen. "See what's there?"

Karen stepped closer, feeling Jane move in behind her. The window had once proudly announced the store as the Heart's Art Gallery in broad curlicue letters. A few months ago, Jane had brought in a painter to add the names of the best-known artists she exhibited. The bullet had clearly pierced the *R* in Karen.

Jane drew in a quick breath, and Karen closed her eyes, a wave of nausea sweeping over her. Who would hate her this much?

Mason muttered the same thing he had earlier at Laurie's. This time it was clearly French and angrier than before.

Karen's eyes snapped open and she scowled. "What?"

Tyler looked at Mason in surprise, then said softly, "Agreed, although she'd never let you get away with it."

Mason's eyebrows shot up, and Tyler shrugged. "I have relatives in Quebec."

"What did you say?" Karen repeated to Mason.

Tyler stood up, inhaling deeply. "Never mind." He looked at Jane. "I'll leave one of the boys on duty here, so nothing walks off. I need all of you to come back to the office with me." He motioned in the general direction of the police station, then moved away.

Karen took Jane's arm and turned to follow Tyler, glancing once over her shoulder at Mason, who was still squatted down next to the plate glass on the ground, staring at it. He opened and closed one fist as if trying to get a hold of something, then beat it against his thigh as he stood.

As if this were his own battle. The thought stilled Karen's rollicking emotions for a moment. Despite the bidding battle he'd had with Luke Knowles, this wasn't truly his fight. This morning, she'd been glad for his friendship, for his support, but now he seemed to have taken the struggle on as his own. She glanced at him again. He'd stopped and his face was turned up toward the sky, his eyes closed.

Is he praying? They had never discussed faith at all. Karen knew he respected hers from the way he reacted when he saw her praying or making time for church activities. But he'd never volunteered anything about his own faith. *Do you believe?*

Jane sniffed, and Karen looked back at her friend, gripping her arm a bit tighter. "Are you okay?"

The young gallery owner shook her head. "I feel…violated." She shivered. "I don't know what to do."

Tyler paused and looked back at her. "You *have* been violated. Most robbery victims feel that way. Plus, you've had things you love destroyed. But you'll have to get back on the horse as soon as you can. I'll get the boys to finish up the evidence work today, so you can start repairs. And I have someone you should talk to. Someone who's been through it."

Jane's eyebrows met, her face reddening. "It can't be that easy."

Tyler shook his head. "It's not. Didn't say it was. It's just something you'll have to do. If you don't, it'll be worse."

The desire to help her friend surged through Karen. "I'll make it up. I'll make all new pieces for you. Something different." She smiled weakly. "Maybe more appealing to the tourists."

Jane's mouth twisted. "Don't you dare make something different," she said, her eyes brightening. "I have enough tourists, thank you very much." The words made both of them grin, and Jane took a deep breath. She gave Karen's arm a quick squeeze. "Thank you. It'll help not having to look at the empty spots."

They paused as Tyler opened the door to the station and held it for them. He waited as Mason ran to catch up, darting in after the women. Peg Madison stepped from behind the front desk and wrapped her arms around Karen and Jane in a tight, motherly hug. "Oh, girls! I'm so sorry!"

Karen adored Peg's hugs. The fiftyish redhead stood almost as tall as her son, and her plush body always sank against the "huggee" like a firm pillow. Karen closed her eyes and took comfort in the embrace, resting her head for a moment against Peg's strong shoulder and inhaling Peg's usual scent of freshly baked bread and the White Shoulders perfume she'd been wearing for the past thirty years. When they released each other, Peg wiped away a tear, then turned her smile on the young man behind them.

"You're Mason." She stepped between Karen and Jane and held out her hand. "I'm Margaret Madison. Peg to everyone but my mother. I can't believe you've been in town this long and I've not met you."

"Yes, ma'am, neither can I." He took her hand. "I've been in and out of town a lot, but I've heard so much about you that I knew we had to meet."

Peg moved closer to him, still holding on to his hand. "All good, I hope," she whispered conspiratorially. Two fingers twisted a lock of hair near her temple.

His smile reflected the conspiracy. "Only the things that can be repeated in public."

Jane leaned toward Karen and whispered, "So does Mason flirt with everyone?"

Peg's eyes flashed at her as she attempted to pull her hand back. "We are not flirting. I'm twice his age."

Mason held firmly to Peg's hand. "I can assure you of two things, Miss Peg. One, you are most definitely *not* twice my age. Two, when Southern boys flirt, age is irrelevant. All that matters is the charm and loveliness of the lady."

Peg cleared her throat as a blush crept up her cheeks, and she eased her hand out of his grip. She returned to her desk as her son watched, arms crossed. She stared back at him. "I assume you're going to take their statements? I set up the tape recorder."

Tyler hesitated a moment, then relented. "Thank you." He led them to his office, a utilitarian space furnished with a well-used metal desk, a filing cabinet and three straight chairs, in addition to his own desk chair. As they sat, he motioned at Mason. "How do you do that so smoothly? I'd trip over my own manners if I tried to speak to a woman like that."

The Louisiana boy shrugged. "Not sure. Mama always said you catch more flies with honey than vinegar, and I've just found most folks like it when you're nice to them. Guess that's something you don't always have the liberty to do."

Tyler shook his head. "Not in this line of work, no." He dug a tape out of his desk, checked to make sure it was rewound, and popped it into the player. He turned it toward them, and nodded again at Mason. "We're not New York up here. None of the flashy stuff you see on television. Just two computers in the whole building, although we do have access to all the national databases. Mostly it's just us and our brains. It gets the job done."

He paused, glancing at Karen. "In a minute, I'm going to separate you in order to ask questions about this morning, but I wanted to say a few things first. I thought the worst part of this would be confined to New York, but it's come home to roost, and I don't want to get caught napping again. I want you to think carefully about the past couple of days, as well as about what you've thought or felt since this started happening. Once the interviews start, leave nothing out, no matter how irrelevant you think it may be. Even the smallest item, especially when combined with other facts, may be significant. Okay?"

Karen sat back in her chair, her stomach tensing again. She avoided Mason's point-blank stare as she spoke. "What does how we *think* have to do with this?"

Tyler leaned back in his chair. "People don't always realize what they know. What I find is often put together from a dozen tidbits from half a dozen sources. Any other questions?"

Jane's black eyes widened, a stark contrast to her pale skin. "Tyler, the shop has been really busy the last two days. Spring brings in the tourists as well as the regulars. Two-dozen folks, maybe more. Laurie came over to talk about some new prints for the café." She glanced at Karen. "Your uncle Jake and aunt Evie were in, buying something for Shane's birthday."

"My cousin," Karen said to Mason.

"I remember. Bald guy. Tanning-bed brown. Big teeth. Keeps popping in for coffee when you're trying to work."

Jane interrupted. "Do you really want to know about everyone who came in the shop?"

Tyler looked from Karen and Mason to Jane. "Jane, we'll talk in another—"

Jane plunged ahead. "They were just normal folks. I mean, as normal as tourists get, anyway." She shrugged. "Most of them are a little whacked. Too much driving. One couple wanted to know if I had any replicas of Grandfather Mountain, and they didn't take kindly to being told that Grandfather Mountain was in North Carolina and that our Old Man in the Mountain had collapsed in 2003. They did buy a quilt."

"Jane…"

"Anyone buy something of Karen's?" Mason asked.

Jane shook her head. "Not yesterday. Sold one last week, but that was to a guy from Miami who comes up here every spring looking for unusual local stuff." She turned to Karen. "You know him. Tall surfer-looking dude, but kinda old. Eddie something. I've spent most of the morning thinking about that auction. How soon can you get those replacements made?"

"That might not be a good idea right now." Tyler leaned forward. "Remember me? I need to talk to you individually. I'm supposed to be in charge here."

"Right. Murder case," Mason blurted.

Jane sat forward, her eyes sharp, her confusion bouncing from Tyler to Mason, whose face reddened as he looked down.

"What murder?" she asked. "What's going on?"

Tyler sighed and explained about Luke Knowles. Jane's shoulders dropped even more as she nodded. "So that's how you knew there'd be a note."

"And why it's important for me to know if you noticed anything peculiar about your customers. While this doesn't have to be someone who knows Karen personally or stays in this area, we shouldn't rule that out, either." He turned to Karen and Mason. "Now, I need you to wait with Peg while I finish with Jane." Tyler cleared his throat, his eyes gentle. "Karen, I know this whole thing might bring up some…unfortunate memories."

In that moment, Karen could have hugged Mercer's young police chief. He might not be the best cop in the world, but he certainly understood his town's residents. She sighed, resigned that her past was going to be a part of this investigation. And that meant that she'd have to tell him about the dream. But that was all right. If anyone in Mercer was going to think she had lost her mind, she'd rather it be Tyler.

Karen shook her head. "No, it's okay. I know it's your job to look at every angle."

The door popped open and Peg stepped in, not waiting for her son to acknowledge her. "I just dispatched two of our officers to Karen's. Her alarm is going off."

FOUR

A roller coaster, Mason thought. This had turned into an out-of-control roller coaster. The image of such a ride, the cars bolting wildly around curves and steep hilly tracks, stuck in Mason's head as Tyler's police cruiser bounced through the short drive to Karen's hillside home. He'd had such car rides before, in other countries with other drivers, but never with this sense of urgency. He and Karen sat in the back, Karen wedged into one corner, her expression bounding from fear to confusion and back again. He reached out to touch her arm. "What are you thinking?" He grimaced immediately, scolding himself for voicing such a stupid question.

The look she gave him, however, held no derision, nor did her response fold around the "Why me?" attitude he half expected from someone going through such persecution.

"I just don't want anyone else to get hurt. First Luke Knowles, now Jane."

"Jane's not—"

Her anguish flooded out. "Her shop is her life, Mason! This hurts her business, her sense of security. She'll be afraid in her own shop!" Karen's voice rose rapidly, ending in a sound close to a sob. "It's clear now that this isn't isolated—that it's me, that he won't stop. And I don't know what he wants!"

Tyler glanced in the rearview mirror. "He wants you to stop making pottery."

Karen slumped. "Yes, I'm sure Laurie could use another waitress. Maybe I could move back in with Aunt Evie and become dependent on others to support me."

Mason drew back, watching her, finally realizing that this cut much deeper than just her work. This was a cut to her soul, her very being. An attack on who she was and the life she'd chosen.

Tyler glanced in the mirror again. "With their resources, I'm sure New York will find out who this is, but we're trying, too."

Karen's chin tipped up, her jaw firm. "And we need to find out why."

Mason glanced from the mirror to the girl and back. Tyler remained silent, his gaze flat and distant as he braked and threw the shift lever into Park.

One of Tyler's officers had already secured the house and waited for them near the front door, which stood open but intact.

The officer noticed Karen's glazed stare. "We came out this way, Ms. O'Neill," he said, looking from her to Tyler. "They went in and out through the basement. Touched nothing upstairs, as far as we can tell, although we've started to fingerprint the doors and windows."

"So the damage is all downstairs?" Tyler asked.

"Yes, sir."

"Where's Lacey?" Karen blurted as she lunged for the house.

The officer blocked her path. "That's the cat?" At Karen's nod, he continued. "We found her hiding upstairs, scared out of her wits. Almost took one of Sergeant Davis's fingers off. He took her to the vet, made sure she was okay."

"Thank you," she whispered, backing away. Without warning, she turned and started down the stone path that led around the house.

Tyler moved quickly to block her way. "Let our guy finish his work. Then we can do the inventory."

Her voice was low and tight. "I need to *see!*"

"Karen …"

Mason stepped up and grabbed her arm. He faced Tyler. "Maybe…if we all went…just so she could look through the door."

The chief hesitated, then gave a curt nod at Karen. "But understand that you cannot go in." He motioned to his officer. "Stay here. Don't let anyone else come close."

The young man touched his hat in acknowledgment, then Tyler led them down and around to the back of the house, taking Karen's other arm as they approached the studio door. Karen tugged forward, surging like a mother toward an endangered child. Mason's grip tightened, his heart aching for her.

"No, Karen," Tyler warned again. "You can't go in until we're finished."

Her breath came in gulps. "Now I know what Jane meant about being violated."

"Easy, *chère*," Mason whispered, desperately wishing he had other words of comfort. He didn't peer inside the house, still focused on Karen.

Tyler spoke softly to the officer. "Have you talked to the neighbors?"

"Not yet," he replied. "Next on the agenda."

"Finished inside?"

"Not quite. It'll be another ten minutes at least, and—" he glanced at Karen "—we'll still need the inventory."

Karen shifted position between the two men and made a noise that was half whimper, half moan. Mason finally looked into the basement door, and his own breath locked in his throat.

The destruction stunned him. The kilns had been tipped over, their firebricks smashed. Completed vases, plaques and bowls had been pulled from the shelves and shattered. The neatly organized baskets of supplies and tools had been ripped from their carefully labeled spots and tossed about the room. Hundreds of hours of work, countless dreams and thousands of dollars. Gone in a mindless rampage.

A fierce rage suddenly knotted Mason's stomach when he saw the wreckage. The words he'd spoken earlier, that had burst from him twice, came to his lips again but this time he swallowed them. It had been a phrase his father had often said about his adventurous, risk-taking mother: "Hide her and keep her."

They had jumped out in his native Cajun patois, and he'd been startled that Tyler had understood. Understood the words, but not the true meaning. Even as a child, Mason had known his father didn't truly want to lock his mother up; instead, he wanted to hold her close, protect her.

"That's what we do…" his father had said "…we

men. Protect our families, in the best way we know how." A frustrating task in a wild country with a wife who liked to wander the swampland, gathering plants for her cooking, and traipse off with her girlfriends to Mardi Gras or a cruise or the occasional trip to Europe. Mason knew for a fact his parents had always been faithful to each other, if strangely mismatched. His father had been content with hearth and home, while Mason's mother, whose pale, Southern-belle beauty contrasted starkly with his father's dark features, had an unquenchable wanderlust—not for other men but for the horizon. She was always leaving. But she always came home.

Mason had inherited both his father's love of the hearth and his mother's wanderlust, a warring combination that had led him to Mercer, but that had made his attraction to this house and this woman almost instantaneous—and disturbing. It was too soon; she was not his to protect. He had no right to the rage that boiled within. This was not his fight.

Yet, somehow, it was. His eyes narrowed, his thoughts going back to the auction as he took a closer look at the demolished studio. *Is this why I found this town, that auction, was the one to go up against Luke Knowles, the one the cops came to first…?*

Mason blinked hard. *No, no, no, I will* not *read hidden meanings into coincidences.*

"No such thing, child. Coincidences are God's sense of timing at work. *You* don't expect it. He does." His mother's words flitted through his head like a persistent moth determined to get inside a lightbulb. No coincidence that a sick friend had given up a ride and hotel room to the young debutante longing to get to her first Mardi Gras. No coincidence that the Cajun boy who'd sworn he'd never attend one had found himself stranded for a week in New Orleans. No coincidence that he'd literally tripped over her in the hotel lobby as she'd checked in, crashing belle and baggage all over the floor, charming her with his chagrin and repeated apologies in Cajun-accented English. His dark, unruly curls and flashing black eyes helped a little, as well...

Mason's mother had never returned to her Birmingham home, transferring to Tulane to finish her business degree. She'd wed the Cajun and started a home business with a new baby on her hip. His mom had loved the story of her romance almost as much as she loved the man himself, and she'd repeated it often to her young son. She would know in her heart that Mason's attraction to Mercer, New Hampshire, and the art of a young potter was no mere "coincidence."

Wish I could tell her. Mason ran his hand through his own curls. He wished he had her faith, her unwavering belief in God's work in their lives. He still missed her. Missed them both.

Mason snapped back to the present as Tyler let go of Karen's arm, and she jerked from Mason's grasp to dash into the house. Mason brushed around Tyler, following as if pulled in by her wake. He stopped dead inside the door, almost running over her. Despite her rush into the house, she stood solid, staring around the basement studio, breathing heavily.

"I'm sorry," Tyler said behind them.

A soft moan sighed out of Karen, and Mason's gaze jerked to her as her knees gave way. He scooped her up, holding her tightly against his chest as the instinctive Cajun phrase burst from him again.

"Hide her and keep her."

Karen's nose twitched as the itch awoke her. She opened her eyes, brushing her fingers over her face, blinking in the one sliver of light not blocked by her closed blinds. A shadowed figure in a chair next to the bed shifted, and her aunt Evie leaned forward. "You okay, girl?" Her quiet voice brought with it a lingering sense of Karen's childhood. Safety, but with a touch of anxiety. As if she were okay, as long as she didn't say the wrong thing.

"I think—" Karen's voice cracked and she cleared her throat. "I think so." She pushed herself up and looked around the darkened bedroom, embarrassment flooding her. "I fainted, didn't I?"

"Yes. You woke up briefly, then fell asleep. Like you were drugged." Her aunt smiled. "Who'd blame you, with all this going on? Why didn't you call us sooner?"

Karen shook her head. "It's happened so fast…" Her voice cracked as her eyes stung with tears. The rage and fear she'd felt downstairs roiled in her again. Her fingers clutched the blanket. "Who would want to hurt—" She stopped as Evie's eyes widened with alarm. The last thing she wanted was Evie on the warpath with this. Evie didn't need more ammunition to use in her criticism of Karen's life. Karen took a deep breath to calm her nerves. "How did I get up here?"

"That boy brought you up. That writer you told me about."

Karen's mouth twisted into a wry smile at both the

answer and how easily Evie had been distracted. "Mason isn't a boy."

Evie snorted. "He's barely more than a baby." The older woman pushed out of the chair, towering over Karen's bed. Her long, salt-and-pepper ponytail swung forward over one shoulder as she leaned over, reaching for Karen's hand. "How do you really feel?"

Karen sighed, sitting up straighter and drawing her knees under her. "To tell you the truth, a little overwhelmed." Her eyes widened as her stomach gave a furious snarl. "What time is it?"

Evie patted her leg. "Obviously time for this girl to eat. It's well after noon. Why don't you come back to the house with Jake and me?"

"I really need to stay here, clean up downstairs."

Evie stiffened. "You want to stay here? After a break-in? You can't be serious."

Pushing back the covers, Karen swung her legs over the edge of the bed. "Of course I am. This is my home."

"You fainted."

"I was stunned."

Evie stepped back out of her way. "You still need to eat. At least let us take you out. That boy can come."

"Mason."

"Mason can come, too."

Karen paused, a little dizzy. "I have food here."

"You shouldn't be alone. Surely you don't plan to have Mason stay over."

Karen felt like shaking off both her sleepiness and this conversation. "We're just friends." She looked around for her shoes, and chose a pair of slip-ons.

"But—"

"Let it alone, please."

Evie sighed. "You and Jake. No blood but equally stubborn under the skin."

Karen ran her fingers through her hair and gave her mascara a quick check in the mirror, smiling as she remembered the morning's conversation. "You're the one who always said persistence was the key to real success."

"In business. Not with family."

"Still, I learned from the best. I don't think Shane learned it from Jake. It was either you or the Army, Evie. Take your pick, but I don't think one tour of duty is long enough for him to have learned business from them."

Evie grinned at the mention of her son's name, brightness showing in her eyes as her concern for her niece gave way to pride in her son. As always. "Did I tell you he sold the old Elkins place? Knew he would. All the other brokers around here kept saying it would never move, but he did it!"

"A tourist with bed-and-breakfast dreams?"

Evie barked a laugh. "Not exactly. Retired couple out of Boston. Name of Carver Billings, I think Shane said. He and his wife have fixed up old houses before, then sold them for quite a profit, and they think this one will be just as easy. Shane closed it as soon as he could. They moved in last weekend."

Karen paused, almost asking if Shane had fully disclosed the house's history to the buyer. The Elkins place was notorious around Mercer: a derelict mansion near collapse, ignored by the locals due to a long history of calamities to the folks who owned it. She decided not to ask, knowing that the answer might lead her back into an even harder conversation about her cousin's business ethics.

"Bad luck," Shane always said, "is not subject to full disclosure." Of course, he never said that in front of Evie.

She forced a smile. "Good for him."

Evie gave a little jig, revealing the grace of her dance training, slowed only slightly by her seventy-plus years. "Full price, too. They didn't even try to negotiate."

"That's great." The last thing Karen wanted to talk about at this moment was her cousin's successes. Evie had always held out Shane—the handsome, successful college graduate—as being everything Karen was not. Like some kind of soap opera cliché, Karen thought as she trotted down the stairs, halting as Mason, her uncle Jake and cousin Shane leaped to their feet. "Wow. Welcoming committee."

Mason moved first, crossing to the foot of the stairs. "You all right?"

No, not really. But I need to do something without everyone looking over my shoulder. "I'm hungry. And I want my house back."

Mason's eyebrows arched. Behind him, Jake grinned, his sunburned face creasing into a thousand crevices. He clapped Shane on the shoulder. "That's our cue to grab the brooms."

"No."

They all froze. "You really want to do this alone?" Jake asked.

Evie began a sputter of protest, but Karen held up her hand. "It's my work. I need to take inventory for the police, to see exactly what was broken. I can't do that with everyone here." She stopped short of saying that the idea of Evie and Shane in her studio made her shudder. They'd made her feel like a second-class citizen as long as she'd lived with them. That was not going to be wiped away in one afternoon of sweeping. She simply didn't want them here.

Mason didn't move, his eyes steady on Karen's face. Shane, however, stepped forward and took one of her hands. He was trim and handsome as always, and his concerned blue eyes gleamed even brighter in a face and scalp evenly tanned by a local studio instead of the sun. Shane had been bald as long as she could remember, but he reveled in it, making him one of the more attractive men around. "Are you sure?" he asked.

When she replied, her voice was quieter but just as determined. "I mean it. I want to eat something from my own kitchen, then just work with Mason to go through what's left of down—" She stopped, realizing she'd just volunteered him for a job he might not relish. She turned to him. "If you want to. I mean, you don't have to, I just thought—"

"Yes."

That was it. Just "Yes," with his gazed locked on her face. After a moment she nodded, then turned to Evie. "I'm glad you were here for me. But I really need to do this myself. I know what was down there—I'll know what's missing."

Evie put up a hand. "I've seen that mess. How could you possibly know what's—"

"Evie girl, let her alone." Jake stepped forward, reached around Karen and took Evie's arm. "This is between her and the clay."

Evie let out a sigh that was a pure picture of exasperation. "Potters! You make me crazy with this thing you have with the clay."

Jake's low chuckle sounded kind, but his grip on Evie's arm didn't loosen. "It's why we do it, sweetheart." He led her out, while Shane squeezed Karen's hand.

"Call me if you need anything. I mean it. Anytime. And we'll talk more later. We have a lot to catch up on."

"Of course."

She closed the door behind them, then turned to Mason. "I think we can—"

"What thing with the clay?"

Karen examined him, but he didn't flinch or waver as her gaze went over him head to toe. He waited, as if understanding her need to decide whether he was serious or about to make fun of her. Yet his eyes held no humor, just curiosity, with his eyebrows arched, his mouth an even line. She remembered the intensity of his first questions about her art, the inquisitiveness that seemed to have no end.

"Come with me." She took his hand and led him down the spiral, stopping only for a second at the bottom as she switched on the lights. She took a deep breath and looked over the room one more time.

The shattered porcelain pieces glimmered under the overhead lights. Her pottery was more than her livelihood; it was her heart. No matter what this…person…wanted, Karen could no more stop creating with clay than she could stop breathing. It was the one thing that her aunt Evie had never understood about her and Jake, no matter how much they'd tried to explain it. Evie's was a world of common sense and practical business, and she never grasped why they *had* to get their hands in the clay, why it drove them…why some part of their soul would be wounded and crippled if they couldn't.

Karen stepped off the staircase, grimacing a bit at the crunch of shards under her shoes, but she didn't stop, picking her way across the room to the tipped wheels. She set the largest one upright, checked it for damage, then made sure it was plugged into the wall. She picked a bat out of one pile and brushed it free of debris before setting it on the wheel's turntable. Then she went to one of her tubs of clay and cut loose a chunk, plopping it with a solid thunk on the worktable. She motioned to Mason, who waited at the stairs. "Get over here and roll this into a ball."

He grinned and followed, brushing his hands on his jeans before attacking the clay. She found two stools and set one behind the wheel, the other in front. She went to the sink for water, poured some over the bat, then put the cup on the wheel's tray. "Bring the clay over here."

He did, and she pointed at the stool behind the wheel. "Sit and get comfy." He settled in, and she took the clay, plopping it firmly on the bat. She sat in front of him and pointed at a spot on his left thigh. "Brace your elbow there. The first thing we do is center the clay. Brace your arm so that your left hand doesn't move. Support the bottom of the clay with it. Then use your right hand to move the clay gently until it's in the center of the bat. Wet your hands, and start the wheel. *Slowly.* You'll know it's centered when it loses its wobble."

She stepped back, watching. He moved clumsily at first, as if he wasn't sure where to place his hands or how hard to push the clay. She giggled when he almost shoved it off the bat, then motioned for him to start over. "Slowly," she repeated.

Once the clay settled into the middle of the bat, she pointed to the cup of water. "Wet your hands and put a bit on the clay, but not too much. You don't want it too moist. Fold your hands around it, then when you're ready, use your thumb to open it up." She watched, fighting her instinct to guide his hands with hers. But as with all her students, especially the younger ones, *doing* had more impact than *showing.*

Mason caught his breath as the clay opened under his hand, almost as a flower opens its petals. She leaned closer, her voice low but intense. "Watch the clay. It'll lead you. Listen to God guiding you. He knows what it should be. Trust your instincts. It's less about what you want to make than what this piece of clay should be."

Karen leaned back then, watching with a teacher's thrill as Mason's eyes focused on the ball of earth in front of him, mesmerized by its spinning growth. The gentle motion of his breathing drew her attention, and she remembered suddenly the lightness in her head earlier that morning, the dizziness that had made her feel as if she were falling…then she *had* fallen, hard, against him. He'd caught her, lifted and carried her up two flights of stairs. His frame might be wiry, but there was a solid strength to his body as well as his mind. She closed her eyes as a tightness clutched her chest. She forced herself to breathe, and a silent prayer raced through her mind. *Lord, not yet. We have too much to handle already. Please don't let me feel this now!*

FIVE

The clay spun beneath Mason's hands, and Karen's words resonated through his head. His gaze locked on the grayish, glistening ball in front of him. Slowly, he bent one finger more than the others, and the clay responded, changing shape as easily as a feather drifts.

Yet there was more. As he caressed the earthen ball, he knew this would be a water jar. It felt intuitive to him, as if he'd held this clay before. A water jar, in fact, like the women carried in biblical times. He moved his hands gently, and the clay reformed, grew.

As an art historian, he knew well what those vessels looked like, but this would be his own creation, as well, inspired by something within him. His hands shifted, and so did the clay, the moist surface of it slick and pliable, yet firm under his touch, spinning steadily, creating a sensation almost like an electric charge beneath his fingertips. One hand formed the wall, pulling it upward, as the outside hand braced the base. Together, his hands lifted, urging the clay higher. The jar grew taller, opening under his hands, a change that awed him.

"Anything beautiful must be handled with care." His father pruned another rosebush, one of a dozen he had planted for his wife.

At seventeen, however, Mason had grown tired of his father's bromides. *"I know girls get hurt easy, Papa. I've already found that out."*

His father looked at him over one shoulder. *"Don't get so smug, boy. Women are stronger than we are. I'm not talking about how girls age or how they hurt. It's beauty that's fragile, and it's more than women or roses. Despite what the poets claim, beauty isn't what you see. It's in your mind."*

A wobble appeared in the clay, an unevenness in the wall of the jar, like a wound. A groan escaped his lips as the jar collapsed in on itself, a ruin of mud and water. He slid his foot off the wheel's pedal, and the spinning stopped.

Mason stared at the clay, and disappointment— almost a sense of loss—seared through him. "What did I do wrong?"

Karen's low voice came from behind him. "'So I went down to the potter's house, and I saw him working at the wheel. But the pot he was shaping from the clay was marred in his hands; so the potter formed it into another pot, shaping it as seemed best to him.'"

He turned toward her, confused. "What?"

She stepped closer, smiling, a broom in one hand where she'd been cleaning. "It's from the Bible. Jeremiah. God knows all about clay." She paused, watching his face. "And those of us who use it. This is your first time at a wheel. This is normal. Sometimes, just the wrong move or touch will make the pot collapse.

Round it and try again. If it does it again, we'll move to different clay. This will be too wet to try a third time."

His eyes still on the wheel, Mason's hands mounded the clay into a ball, checked the centering as she'd instructed, and started again. Yet something had changed in his mind, in his view of the water jar. It formed smaller this time, with a more delicate look but a thicker wall, almost like a deep bowl. It grew, reshaped and matured under his fingers. Time vanished as his mind, eyes, all his senses focused on the creation before him. The smell of damp earth filled his nostrils, and he heard only the whirl of the wheel. His fingers seemed melded to the clay, as if he'd become bonded to it.

Beauty is in the mind. It's in the act. It had been in the face of a man who'd broken away from his only son to dash into a blazing house after the woman he'd loved for twenty years. Mason would never forget the look or the act. It was the last thing his father did.

Karen took his right hand and placed a stylus in it, and he used the point to insert fine lines around the upper edge. Finally, he lifted his hands away and straightened, a bit startled that his back ached. He twisted a bit to stretch his muscles, his eyes still on the clay. Yet he knew it was finished. The clay had become what it was meant to be. Satisfied, he took his foot off the pedal. As the jar slowed to a halt, his eyes narrowed. Returned to reality, he saw that the jar looked like a young child's art project, its too-thick walls a bit crooked, the lines around the neck far from straight. Yet...

"Very nice."

He jumped. He'd forgotten that Karen was still in the room. He shook his head. "It looks...lumpy."

Her laughter brightened the air around them. "It's *still* your first time on a wheel. I think it's amazing."

Mason finally looked away from the jar, first to her, then to windows behind him. The light had faded to a dim evening purple. Mason stood suddenly, tipping over the stool, his gaze flashing about the room.

The basement studio had changed dramatically. Karen had righted all the equipment and many of the baskets and supplies had been restored to their previous order. Shards of fired and raw clay had been swept into a half-dozen piles of like colors—red and black in one pile, blue and yellow in another. A rust and bronze stack of broken raku-fired pieces stood near the door.

Mason's jaw dropped. "How long—"

"About ninety minutes." Her grin sparkled. "I even grabbed a snack while you were working. Now you get it. The thing with the clay."

His words stuck in his throat, and Karen waited patiently, leaning on her broom. Mason's mind spun, like the wheel, as he tried to get a grip on what just happened. He had not heard her sweeping or moving anything. He'd had no idea that much time had passed. His time on the wheel had felt brief, miniscule, no longer than a song on the radio. The feel of the clay, the rotations of the wheel, had sucked him in, mesmerized him. The world had closed in around him, confined to the circle of water and earth. All existence had narrowed to the creation of a water jar.

Karen shifted her weight from one foot to the other, and her voice dropped, barely more than a whisper. Still, in the rock, plaster and glass of her studio, her words were clear. "It doesn't happen to everyone. Aunt

Evie, who was an efficient nurse and is now a dance teacher with all the patience in the world with her students, can't get beyond the icky feeling of the clay. Jane, who loves art and artists, can make a pretty pot, but it doesn't capture her. For her, it's just a chore that puts her manicures at risk. She embraces art but can't 'do' art. That's why she sells it."

"That's why I'm a historian who teaches and writes about art." His hoarseness surprised him, and he cleared his throat. "I can't 'do' it either."

Karen nodded at the lopsided water jar. "Oh, yes, you can. My guess is you just had not found which art is yours. Maybe the way you got lost is a sure sign that you have now." She took a deep breath and leaned the broom against a shelf. She leaned against the same shelf and crossed her arms. "No one thought I could do it, either." She looked down at the floor, her gaze distant. "After my parents died, I became a wild child. Aunt Evie couldn't do anything with me. I lost focus on everything. I barely passed any of my classes. Counselors, ADHD medications…nothing worked." She paused. "When I turned fifteen, I asked Jake if he could help me with an art project, and instead he introduced me to the wheel. Four hours later I had a pot and a new way to focus. From that day, everything changed. When I couldn't study, I'd go to his studio…then I could go back to the books."

She looked at him, the blue in her eyes so dark and intense that Mason felt the impact of her gaze all the way to his toes. "Jake also brought me to God. You have no idea how wild I was. How out of control. How many times I'd already been in court. I really was on a path of no return. Only the grace of God and a good-hearted judge kept me from having a juvenile record." She waved away her past. "I believe God saved my life the first time, with my parents, then the clay saved my life later. Jake gave me the Scripture that says, 'Then the word of the Lord came to me: "O house of Israel, can I not do with you as this potter does?" declares the Lord. "Like clay in the hand of the potter, so are you in my hand."' And," she continued softly, "Jake reminded me that an artist of any medium has been granted an incredible gift from God. It's on loan from Him. Our hearts long to give it back to Him in the same way we crave Him. It's not just what we do for a living." She took a deep breath and let it out slowly. "God's intervention. I won't stop. I can't."

The pressure in Mason's chest threatened to choke off his breath. His mind still felt oddly out of sync, a bit numb and not quite back in the real world. Yet this amazing woman had captured his heart, and his earlier need to protect her intensified, even as his respect for her work, her heart, her past, soared. She was both the strongest woman he'd ever met…and the most fragile. He straightened, stretching a kinked muscle in his back.

"Then I don't think you should." He almost smiled at the relief in her face, but he continued. "But I also am not convinced that you should stay here tonight."

"This is my home. I won't abandon it."

Mason stood and walked to the sink, organizing his argument as he washed the clay from his hands.

The clay. He watched the muddy water swirl down the drain, realizing she'd shared her most intimate world with him. Her home. Her clay. She might still be holding him at arm's length, but what she had shared spoke straight to his soul.

He dried his hands and went to her, raising her fingers and kissing them lightly. "These hands," he said softly, "let your soul shine through your art. This person is determined to stop you, so he has made your house a target because it's not secure. If you stay somewhere safe, there is hope he might leave the house as well as you alone."

"I won't go to Aunt Evie's."

Mason didn't question her determination to avoid her childhood home. She'd said it twice. That was enough. Explanations could come later. "Then I have an idea…."

An hour later a car pulled up in front of Karen's house. Large, powerful and a nondescript charcoal gray. In the twilight, even the make and model were a mystery. The tall, lanky man who unfolded from the driver's seat, however, stood out because of both his height and the Eurasian cast of his features and skin. Fletcher MacAllister greeted the two young people with a wave and a scowl. "You missed dinner," he said to Mason. "Maggie's not a happy camper."

Karen snickered as Mason tried not to look too embarrassed. Fletcher's wife, Maggie, managed Jackson's Retreat, the writers' colony where Mason had lived for the past few months. Even the locals were familiar with most of the rules of the retreat, including the one that stated that all residents, without exception, ate their evening meal in the main lodge.

"Think she'll forgive me?"

Fletcher picked up the bag Karen had at her feet and

put it in the trunk. "Under the circumstances, probably. Just don't make a habit of…" Fletcher's voice trailed off and he grew still, his eyes scanning the front and side of Karen's home. He wandered toward the stone path at the side, leaving the trunk open. He walked slowly, his gaze moving over the ground as if he were tracking animals.

"Fletcher?" Mason asked.

Karen put a hand on his arm, her voice a low whisper. "Just wait."

They followed as Fletcher headed for the back, stopping as he examined the back door. He squatted, examining the door frame. "No forced entry?"

"No."

Mason glanced at her, then cleared his throat. "Tyler didn't get a chance to talk to Karen about—"

Fletcher ran a finger down the edge of the door. "I know. I called him when you asked me if Karen could stay for a while at the retreat. He filled me in, asked if I would… You have a key outside?"

Karen nodded. "Yes, but it's hidden."

Fletcher backed up, then looked around the area near the door, taking in every detail. Finally he reached down and turned over a rock about four feet from the walk. The key's brass color shone stark against the dark earth.

Karen's frustration rose in her throat. "How did you—"

"It's been moved. The rock, I mean. How many people know you have a key out here?"

"Family. Maybe a couple of friends. You know, I forget sometimes you were a New York cop."

Fletcher turned, a crooked grin on his face. "I'm

glad. Wish I could. And I know there are times Maggie wishes I could stop. Anyone else?"

Karen paused, running through the list of people she trusted enough to share the key's location. Jane, who wouldn't tell a soul. Aunt Evie. Jake. Shane. Then, "Oh."

Fletcher and Mason came alert, speaking at the same time. "Who?"

Karen sighed, then bent to pick up the key. "Last year I had some work done, some refinishing in the house. Had all the windows installed. The general contractor on the job knew about the key. Some of his workers might have seen him pick it up."

Fletcher glowered. "And you didn't change the locks or the hiding place?"

Her eyes widened. "It's Mercer!"

"It's also 2008." Mason ended the sentence with a slight growl.

Karen, suddenly annoyed at both of them—and herself—propped her hands on her hips, defiant. "Don't patronize me."

Fletcher went back to studying the ground around the door. "Did anyone but Tyler know you were going to breakfast?"

"No, and I'm not usually out of the house so early in the morning. It's some of my best work time. The light in the studio is amazing in the morning." Karen sighed, not quite believing all that had happened in just one day. "I get my best ideas, just looking out over the yard, thinking, maybe pray—"

"So if this were planned, they had to be watching or know you'd be gone."

"How could they—"

"Jane's!" Mason's word burst out across the yard.

"Give the man a cigar," Fletcher murmured.

Karen's stomach churned. "You think that was to get me out of the house?"

"Guaranteed." The Cajun accent in Mason's drawl caused Fletcher and Karen to turn to him. Mason nodded. "It would guarantee that both Karen and Tyler would be occupied. What else would?"

Fletcher nodded absently. "Tyler should put you on a consultant's retainer the way he has me."

Karen grinned at Mason's puzzled look and whispered, "I'll explain later." Karen loved telling Fletcher's story, as many of Mercer's natives did. They were fascinated by the tall detective, who had adopted their town and married one of their favorite residents, Maggie Weston. Bestselling author Aaron Jackson, who had started the writers' colony, was Fletcher's best friend, and Aaron had used Fletcher as the model for his hero in a series of novels. This had brought a lot of uncomfortable fame to the introspective investigator, and it was part of the reason Fletcher had left the NYPD. Fletcher had no interest in sharing his private life with Aaron's fans, a reluctance that, of course, made them even more curious. After Aaron's murder, Fletcher had put his NYPD training to work to assist Tyler in the investigation. In the process, he'd fallen hard for Maggie, only adding to his charm for the local folks.

Fletcher rotated slowly, his focus now turned away from the house, his gaze scanning through the trees and down the back slope. He pointed at a trail that led away through the trees. "Where does that go?"

"It crosses Oak Drive about a quarter mile from here,

then skirts the city park and ends up at the old Elkins place. I use it to get to Aunt Evie's on Oak and to jog in the park."

"Do a lot of folks know about it?"

"Pretty much the whole town." She pointed back at her basement. "The original owner here died before the house was finished, but his wife kept kids after school for almost a year, trying to pay the bills. Once local kids find out about a trail like this, it's never a secret again."

"Kids," Fletcher muttered, then turned away again. Karen almost burst out laughing. For a couple of months rumors had been circulating that Maggie might be pregnant...rumors that had started when Maggie had joined a knitting class and started stocking up on lots of light blue and pink yarn. Looking at his back, Karen hoped the reticent detective would not be surprised by the boisterous way Mercer, and in particular Maggie's church, welcomed a new baby into their midst.

"Do the kids still use it much?" Fletcher walked closer to the tree line.

"Occasionally. More often during the school year, cutting between the neighborhoods and downtown. I gave a few lessons last summer in the high school art classes, and the kids from the class sometimes drop by to see what I'm doing these days." Karen paused, her eyes widening. "You don't think this was a kid!"

He shook his head, staring at the ground. "No, but I do think this is how whoever did it got away. I wanted to know how cluttered the trail might be." He pointed at the ground. "Clay dust."

Karen and Mason rushed to his side and Mason squatted. "I'll be. Clear as day."

Fletcher shrugged. "Well, not all that clear. But from the description Tyler gave me of your basement, my guess is that the guy walked out covered in it." He looked again at the woods. "If we're lucky, he had a few shards that clung to him, as well, maybe dropped off along the way. If we find a suspect with clay dust on his clothes, we'd have something to compare. With the alarm, he knew he didn't have much time, so he had to break in and get out in about three minutes. Enough time to destroy but not enough time to clean himself up. I'll get Tyler's guys back over here to secure the trail tonight. We'll look tomorrow."

Mason looked up at him. "So you're convinced this is a man?"

Fletcher tilted his head sideways. "Almost certain." He let out a long breath and looked down at Karen. "What's worse, I think it's probably someone you know."

Karen shook her head, backing away from him. "I can't accept that, Fletcher. No one I know would do this!"

Fletcher looked her up and down, his brown eyes intense. "Women who have conflict with people they know tend to lie, scheme, betray. They plot. They don't usually turn to violence, and when they do, it makes the evening news because it's so rare. Men are more likely to take action, even against people they care about. This is someone who knows your art, your home, your routine. He knew your studio was in your home, which room it was in and how to get you out of the house. He either knows you or has been watching you."

Mason's blunt voice cut in. "Which is why I want her out of the house."

Fletcher's eyebrows went up, and he brushed away a smile with his hand. "So let's get to it."

Karen stared at Mason as a twinge formed in her gut that was part annoyance—what right did he have to tell her what to do?—and part affection. *I can't believe he wants to protect me like this.* She spun away from them both. "Give me a minute, okay?"

She heard them head back up the stone path, but she kept her gaze on the woods behind her house. Just that morning she'd watched the sun ease above the trees, filling her world with glorious light. Now, as it sank on the other side of the house, the woods felt unexpectedly ominous. A breeze moved through the trees, lifting her hair and pushing the leaves to a soft whisper.

Memories of times in those woods flowed through her mind. They were one reason she'd wanted this house so much. She and Penny Elkins darting through them, chasing squirrels and the occasional deer. With fallen tree limbs they'd built towering mansions and sleek airplanes, great ocean liners and successful restaurants. The grand dreams of children.

Then, without warning, her memory flashed red and white, bright, explosive colors. Karen gasped and jerked back to reality. "What in the world…" Her voice trailed off as she tried to process the thoughts of red and white. Swirls spun, and the white clustered into clouds, the red fading to a gentle blue. The sky. But why…?

She stood stock-still. This had happened before, these flashes, which one of her childhood therapists had claimed were repressed memories. She didn't quite believe it, but now…

Karen spun and went back to the house, digging the key

out of her pocket. She flung open the basement, deactivated the alarm and grabbed a box from one of the shelves. Moving rapidly, she filled it with brushes, glazes and tools.

"What are you doing?" Mason asked from the doorway. "We were getting wor—"

She pointed to a box on one of the bottom shelves. "Grab that clay."

"What's going on?" He picked up the box.

Karen tossed a sketch pad into her box, then paused just long enough to tap the side of her head. "Something—a memory, I think—is trying to push through. I have no idea what it is, but when it comes, I want to be ready."

Luke Knowles's client watched silently as Karen re-emerged from her basement, pottery supplies in hand and that idiotic professor in tow. A low snarl seeped from between clenched teeth, and a hand brushed back a tree branch as the two headed up the stone path and disappeared into Fletcher MacAllister's car.

Then the snarl eased into a long sigh of frustration.

Why is she so stubborn? It should have been over by now!

She had to stop making those freakish vases. Jumpy and unfocused, that was her typical manner. So easily distracted. Surely the three coordinated hits—Knowles, the gallery, her home—would be enough to convince her to move in other directions with her wretched pots. The plan had been so simple; scare her, distract her. Kill her? Yes, the thought had occurred. But the time was not right. Not yet. Maybe later, when the gain had been firmly secured.

DuBroc and MacAllister's involvement added unforeseen complications. Both were outsiders and would be quick to spot problems that locals might not notice…like someone being in these woods, watching. Worries about Tyler Madison had been nonexistent—this was way out of his league. He and his men hadn't even looked at the woods. And even if they'd seen the familiar face peering at them, they wouldn't have thought twice about it.

Dolts, all of the local ones. But MacAllister had turned to the woods immediately, almost as if he could see the outline of the watcher still hanging about to see the results of his handiwork. His remaining ties to the NYPD could also prove troublesome. He trusted no one. Meanwhile, DuBroc's hovering could give Karen a useless sense of security, while his adoration of those awful vases could give her the encouragement to "buck up and carry on." That she had gone back for supplies and clay…definitely not a good sign.

Not good at all.

The bark of a maple tree pushed through the client's shirt as shoulders pressed back, a weariness settling over them. *I never wanted this to get so bloody. Please let her get the message soon.*

Care had to be taken, but the path was set. There was no choice. She had to stop. Or be stopped.

SIX

Karen stood silently as Fletcher and Mason unloaded the car, looking up at the A-frame lodge house. Already she missed her home, her own bed. Lacey. Still, this was better than going to Evie's.

The locals just called it "The Retreat." Most of them didn't even know its official name: The Aaron Jackson Foundation Writers and Artists Colony of Mercer, New Hampshire. They would have snorted at the pretentiousness of such a title, anyway. After all, it wasn't a resort, just a cluster of cabins scattered over ten acres of rolling woodland. The center of the retreat, the rustic four-bedroom lodge, was the most impressive part of the estate and was home to a groundskeeper and the retreat's manager, Maggie, along with her husband, Fletcher MacAllister.

The local folks might have sighed a bit, however, to know that the "Foundation" part of the title had been added by Maggie after Aaron Jackson's death the year before. Aaron had founded the retreat as his literary legacy, and then had been murdered on the lodge's back deck. Aaron had been a vibrant character, flamboyantly prowling Mercer's cafés and galleries, supporting the region's artists and writers and the town itself out of the proceeds from his detective novels. Fletcher, the model for the hero of those novels, exuded an unusual magnetism, and the respect and affection he showed toward his wife reminded Karen that there were, in fact, still men about who deserved the title of gentleman.

The thought made her glance toward Mason, who stood, eyes down, as Maggie berated him for breaking one of the key rules of the retreat.

"There are too many people here dedicated to making this work for their careers, Mason, and too many who want to be here." The strands of Maggie's soft auburn hair trembled around her face as she spoke. "I understand everyone has a problem now and then, but you've been distinctly absent the past few days. If you can be successfully productive somewhere else, then you don't need us. What have you written this week?"

Fletcher set Karen's suitcase and box of supplies down at her feet, then straightened, watching Maggie, his weight resting on one foot. Karen wondered if he felt what she did—a strong desire to interrupt, to defend Mason's actions in light of the day's events. But they both remained quiet, markedly aware that this was between Mason and Maggie. When she finally paused, Mason cleared his throat, his voice soft.

"Do you remember when Aaron was working on his fourteenth novel? When he suddenly stopped, set it aside and started a brand-new one?"

Maggie stepped back, clearly not expecting this defense, but willing to go along. "I do. He'd taken a vacation to Bon Aire and become fascinated with scuba diving. He got back and couldn't let it go, so he went back, stayed another month and started a new book about the island and diving."

"It launched as his fourteenth book. He finished the other one later."

Maggie nodded. "And?"

"I'm fascinated by Karen's pottery." Mason's face lit up, his enthusiasm almost childlike in its glee. "From the moment I saw the vases in Jane's gallery," he continued, "I knew I had to follow my nose, so to speak. I'm known for my research about art crimes, but part of what I do is find the best new artists and make sure they become better known. And here were these vases…they were the most creative body of work I'd come across in a long time. Then to find out that the potter lived here…well, the second art crime book has been a bit sidetracked."

Maggie's vivid green eyes swung slowly to Karen, and her lips pursed, as if she were fighting a smile. "Ever been the object of an obsession before?"

Karen's cheeks felt parched by the heat of embarrassment. She opened her mouth, but it was Fletcher who answered. "Probably not twice in one day."

The thought sobered them all, and Maggie let out a long breath, her gaze back on Mason. "All right. But I can't make exceptions for you too much longer." She shook a slender finger at him. "No matter what the circumstances."

Mason nodded. "I understand."

"Good." She turned to Karen. "Would you rather stay in the house or in one of the cabins?"

Mason and Fletcher chimed in with a simultaneous masculine chorus. "House."

Maggie straightened her spine and arched her neck,

bringing her chin down. Her eyes narrowed and seemed to harden, reminding Karen distinctly of Lacey about to pounce on her chosen prey. Her voice dropped, making the words a low and somewhat threatening rumble. "I don't believe I addressed either of you."

Karen choked on a smidgen of laughter and swallowed heavily as both men took a slight step backward and looked away from them. "I'm most concerned about a place to work, where I can put my wheel, maybe a kiln. If I can't go back to my own house until this is over, I'll need them here. They'll need a solid floor, preferably concrete, a 220 plug and a source of water."

Maggie nodded, apparently distracted from her urge to flay two overprotective men. "We can set that up in the studio." At Karen's puzzled look, Maggie lifted one shoulder in a half shrug. "We're thinking about opening residency up to artists as well as writers, but the cabins aren't set up to store great quantities of supplies. After all, an eight-by-eight-foot canvas takes up a lot more space than a laptop computer. So we built a studio last year. Lots of windows and spots for the larger canvases. It's wired and there's a sink with a paint trap. It's also not too far from the lodge, which would make both of these pups happy."

Karen nodded. "That should work fine." She sighed. "I really appreciate this, Maggie. This morning when I got up, I certainly didn't expect—"

Maggie cut her off with a wave of her hand and walked closer, stroking Karen's shoulder. "It's no imposition, I promise. Besides, I know all too well how upside down your life can get in one day." She bent to pick up the suitcase at Karen's feet, only to have

Fletcher leap toward it, reaching the handle before she could grasp it. Maggie straightened, scowling at him. "I'm not an invalid, you know."

A rush of joy shot through Karen, and she almost squealed. "So it's true!" She grabbed Maggie's arms, startling the older woman. "Isn't it?"

Maggie froze for a moment, annoyance knitting her eyebrows together. Then she relented, her shoulders dropping a bit, and nodded. "Yes," she said softly.

Karen pulled her into a hug, which Maggie returned warmly, enveloping them both in the comfortable aroma of Maggie's ever-present sandalwood perfume. "Congratulations!"

"Thank you. We weren't going to tell anyone yet, but…"

"It's a very small town," Fletcher finished, amusement in his voice and eyes.

Karen released her friend. "When?"

"Around Christmas, we think."

"Awesome!" Karen bounced up on her toes. "This actually means my day ends on a good note."

Maggie's eyes widened. "If I'd known it would help this much, I would have told you sooner."

"No, this is perfect. I needed it now. And I'll help any way I can when the time comes," Karen promised. "I love babies!"

"Believe me, I'll remember that the first time I need a babysitter." Maggie turned and took Mason's arm. "Now, I know for a fact you two haven't eaten, and I may scold my writers, but I never let them go hungry." She tugged him toward the kitchen. "I saved two plates from supper. All they need is a little heat from the microwave."

Fletcher set Karen's suitcase down again and offered her his arm. "Suitcases can wait. Let's eat. Miss O'Neill?"

She grinned and slipped her hand into the crook of his elbow. "My pleasure, Mr. MacAllister."

Two hours later, with dinner finished and the kitchen tidy, Karen unpacked in one of the spare rooms of the lodge. She got ready for bed, then lay back across the mattress, staring at the ceiling, going over the events of the day one more time. The early morning, with its crisp air and warm coffee, felt like a year away, almost like a favorite memory that had suddenly become hard to recall. Thoughts of Luke Knowles, Jane's shop and the destruction in her studio followed, renewing the sharp ache that had made a home just below her heart and stayed there all day. Even watching Mason with the clay—he had been so *captured* by the formation of the earth beneath his hands—could not hold the joy it should have for long.

A long, slow breath eased out of Karen as tears stung the corners of her eyes. "Lord, why is my life changing so much? Is this part of Your plan or interference with what You want for me? First Mason, now all this?" Frustration roiled over her. *Why is this happening?* How on earth could those vases mean anything to *any*body other than as a piece of artwork? People sometimes developed emotional attachments to objects, but these were usually pleasant feelings because they either had made it, or had received it from someone special.

So…what did they mean?

The thought made Karen sit up, scowling. "Not a good emotion," she murmured. "Someone who hates not me but the vases themselves." What would make someone *hate* an object?

Bad memories, surely, but why?

Karen stood and went to the window. The bedroom Maggie had assigned her overlooked the wooded acres behind the lodge where the cabins lay scattered. She could see only three of the ten buildings, two cabins and the studio where Fletcher had stored her supplies. The larger of the two cabins was the home of a writer who'd been at the retreat for more than a year. The smaller one, just to the left of the studio, was Mason's. A light still shone in one of the windows, casting a warm gold over the ground outside. She could see him moving about rapidly, almost as if he were pacing.

A gentle smile spread over her face. "What a mess we are," she whispered. "You've touched my heart, Mason DuBroc. But why did this happen now? And why are you even here?"

Why, indeed. Karen returned to the bed and sat down heavily, closing her eyes, murmuring, "Lord, help us. I *so* need Your wisdom and guidance. I don't know what any of this means, this horror with the vases, these feelings for Mason. I don't even know what to do next. Help?" Then, as was her custom, she waited.

It was what Jake had taught her, almost as a part of her training with the clay. "Prayer is a two-way conversation, child. You have to talk. You have to listen. Just like with me." It hadn't just been Jake's lesson on pottery that had helped her focus her riotous brain; it had also been his lessons on prayer.

Karen breathed deeply, evenly, eyes still closed. Listening. Slowly, a sense of peace settled over her, as one of her pottery lessons with Jake floated through her mind. She'd been nervous about trying to do something different, unique, with her art, instead of routine pieces that might sell locally, but not truly reflect her vision. Jake had reached out, picked up a lump of clay and dropped it in her hand.

"God gave you this. He trusted you with this precious gift. Trust Him to guide your use of it. You are His child. He will protect you."

Karen's eyes snapped open. "Protect *me? But…*"

Trust.

"Always the hard part, that trusting," Jake frequently reminded her. *"We humans want to do our own thing, control our own lives, go our own way. Some say it's natural, but it's not. Gotta be His way or it never works like it should."*

Trust.

Karen stood up and finished getting ready for bed. "Okay, Lord," she said, slipping between the sheets. "I know You're there. You've given me too many blessings over the years to doubt. Just let me know what I need to do." Snuggling down, she drifted off into a sleep of pure exhaustion.

That night, the nightmares returned.

"She woke us all up screaming. She's been like this ever since, so we called Jake."

Mason froze in the door frame, one foot in the main room of the lodge, the other still on the back deck. Maggie and Fletcher turned to look at him, then Fletcher nodded for him to come over.

He had awakened suddenly, needing to see Karen, to know she was safe. He'd walked over from his cabin to see if Karen wanted to go get breakfast. It was still early, barely 6:00 a.m., but he knew that both Maggie and Karen were early risers, and the lights in the lodge house already blazed brightly. But Maggie's words had not exactly brought a warm welcome.

The front wall of the great room had a large fireplace in the middle, with an intricately carved, dark wood mantel, around which a seating area had been arranged. Karen sat on one of the plush couches, a quilt around her shoulders, her feet tucked up next to her hips on the cushions. Her pale face looked drawn and tight, and her eyes seemed to be focused on something not of this world.

Fletcher and Maggie stood next to her, Maggie clinging to Fletcher's arm. They were all still in their pajamas and robes, although Maggie had managed to make coffee. Fletcher and Karen both held on to cups as if afraid the coffee would fly away at any moment. Jake sat on the sofa next to Karen, clutching her hand. "How long has it been?" His low voice had a rough, steely edge to it. "I know you were still having them when you left home. So…ten years?"

Karen remained still a moment, then blinked and nodded.

Mason knelt in front of her. "They stopped when she started making the vases."

Karen eased back to awareness at his words, her gaze coming into focus. Her eyes focused on him, and she collapsed toward him, throwing off the quilt and sliding off the couch into his arms. "What does he want from me!"

Startled, Mason caught her, wrapping his arms around her. Her anguished cry wrenched his heart, and he held her silently, clueless as to what to do next. Looking over her shoulder at the older man, he could see Jake nodding at Maggie. "This is progress," he said, the rumbling growl of his voice a little lighter.

They waited until Karen's tears subsided. Mason felt adrift, uncertain of what to do or say, yet oddly thrilled that she'd turned to him in such an intimate moment. His arms tightened, and he closed his eyes as he took in her gentle scent of sleep and flowers. More than anything, he wanted to make her pain go away. And never let her go.

Yet as the sobs eased, she pushed away from him, her eyes downcast. "This is embarrassing," she murmured.

The old man on the couch slapped his leg and leaned forward. "Nonsense, girl! Nightmares are some of the most terrifying experiences we can have. I've seen grown men squall like babies after having rough ones." He leaned back against the couch. "Might have even been known to shed a few tears over them myself."

Karen glanced briefly at Mason's face, then down again. She plucked at his shirt. "I got you all wet."

"It'll dry." He gently pushed the wayward strands of her hair away from her face. "What can I do to help?"

She shook her head. "I'm not sure anyone can do anything." Karen looked around at Maggie and Fletcher.

Jake was more positive. "Of course they can, child. Just give us the chance." He looked at each of them. "Now. What do we do about Miss Karen here?"

"I *am* still in the room," Karen muttered, more color returning to her cheeks.

"Which leads us to the first question. What do *you* want to do?" Jake motioned for Karen to get back on the couch. "Get up here where we can look at you."

She did, her face pinched in thought, and Jake wrapped her in the quilt again.

Fletcher cleared his throat. "All of these actions seem aimed at terrifying you. Scaring you so you'll stop making the face vases. Let's skip the why for a moment in favor of a firm decision. Do you want to stop making them?"

Karen shook her head. "I don't think I *can* stop. The nightmares stopped years ago *only* after I started making them. Obviously my brain is giving me fair warning that they'll come back if I quit." She looked around, her lips a thin line, a serious stubbornness coming back into her eyes. "Besides, I don't want this person to win. That would leave me in fear the rest of my life—that there's someone out there with that much anger toward me. Even if I stopped, that person will still be out there!"

Fletcher nodded. "Yes, but you know if you don't stop, this whole business could get a lot worse before we find out who's responsible."

"Which brings us back to the why." Mason stood up. "I'm wondering if your brain is not also telling you that this isn't random. That this is not just some nut with a problem with your vases. That it is, in fact, connected with whatever is causing your nightmares."

"I don't want it to be," Karen whispered, looking defeated. "It can't be."

"Hmph." Jake let out a frustrated grunt. "Look at me, girl."

Karen did.

"Now. You want to tell them or shall I?"

No one moved for a moment, then Karen looked down at the floor, her shoulders drooping. Jake looked up at Fletcher and Maggie. "From the first nightmare, I believed we both knew who she was seeing. It's one of the reasons why we fought so hard to find a way to make them stop. The face in her dream is the face of the person who killed her parents."

SEVEN

As Jake spoke, Mason watched Karen turn more and more inward, hugging the quilt around her shoulders like a child afraid of the dark—or her dreams. He could relate, given the nightmares he'd had after his own parents' deaths. *We have more in common than we realized, my dear Karen.*

Jake's voice broadened, dropping into the clear, light cadence of a gifted storyteller as he recalled the background of the murder. "David and Stephanie were typical children of the sixties. They traveled all over the country in an old minibus, hitting concerts and rock festivals before spending time in a commune outside San Francisco. That life eventually wore thin for both of them, native-born Mercer kids that they were. They returned home in the seventies, after David's father passed away and left him the family farm."

He reached out and took Karen's hand, trying to pull her into the conversation. "Do you remember anything from the time at the farmhouse?"

She shook her head, her eyes still distant. "I barely remember that there *is* a farmhouse."

Jake hesitated, wetting his lips. Then he looked up

at the others again. "David loved the farmhouse, always had, and Stephanie took to their new home life with gusto. Stephanie started a little home business with her fruit and vegetable canning, and David went into real estate. Karen was born a few months after David completed his real estate courses. Turned out the man the old farmers around Mercer called 'that hippie boy' had quite a talent for business. Stephanie put her energies into her daughter and her little side business. They rejoined the church they'd grown up in and became deeply involved in the community."

He paused again, checking Karen to see how she was handling his narrative. She remained in her own world, and Mason sat down on the other side of her. He took her hand, which remained limp in his palm.

"They put down roots that were New England deep, and seemed to live an incredibly normal life. This is a small town. We all know each other. They were home-grown kids. Everyone was stunned by their deaths."

Fletcher crossed his arms. "Which is one reason why people think the murders had to be connected to David's business. It couldn't have been local or someone would have seen it coming." At Mason's and Jake's looks of surprise, Fletcher tilted his head to one side and nodded at Karen. "When I moved to Mercer, Tyler asked me to look over the files on every unsolved crime since 1970. This one kinda stood out."

Karen snapped back to the present, glaring up at him, then Jake. "Yeah, I guess double homicides don't come along every day."

"Karen, I just meant—"

She held up a hand to interrupt him. "Never mind,

Fletcher. I— Just never mind." With that, she tugged the quilt tighter and retreated into herself again.

In the silence that followed, Mason squeezed her hand. This time, she returned the gesture. He took a deep breath. "Jake, since you're telling us all this, you must think it's local, someone they knew, not business."

Jake shrugged, but Fletcher stepped in. "The problem is that the crime scene information makes it look personal and more about Stephanie than David. But if it were about Stephanie, or both of them, it's a rather remarkable bit of timing. You would have to know that David was in the house, which, admittedly, was no great feat. Open houses are advertised widely. But if this were about Stephanie, then the killer would also have to know that she would be there, as well." He paused. "It's actually pretty ingenuous, if you think about it. It looks like a random robbery gone bad. Open houses aren't strangers to crime. And it makes gathering evidence a nightmare of conflicting finger- and footprints, not to mention trace evidence like hairs and DNA samples. You'd have to eliminate every person who'd been in that house since it had gone on sale."

Jake nodded. "In the mid-eighties, Mercer wasn't exactly a hotbed of crime scene technology." He shrugged. "Still isn't." At Mason's frown, he went on. "Just ask Tyler. I sit on the city council, and he's been begging for more equipment since he took the job."

Fletcher looked at Mason, then Karen. "Given what they knew at the time, I can see why they drew the conclusions they did, and got nowhere. David appeared to be a scrupulously honest businessman, and he and his family were just in the wrong house at the wrong time. Random. Unsolvable."

Mason spoke slowly, recognition finally dawning. "Except for what Karen saw."

Karen shuddered and looked up at him. "I don't know that I *saw* anything. I may have been in the backyard." She turned to stare at Jake. "That's why I can't be nearly as certain as you that the face in my dreams is the murderer."

He shook his head. "You were too traumatized. Memory repression is not something the mind does lightly or easily." He touched the side of her head gently. "Our minds are curious creations. We take in so much, storing it carefully. Children can witness horrible things and remember—car wrecks, war. We learn, we teach, we absorb. You saw something your brain couldn't accept. To your mind, it was an absolute impossibility. Yet it happened."

Karen sat a little straighter. "What do you suggest I do?"

Fletcher tilted his head sideways as he looked at her, curiosity in his eyes. "Where do your earliest memories take place?"

"Home." She paused, shaking her head. "Not the farm. Aunt Evie's. I don't remember the farm at all."

"Have you ever been to the farm?" Maggie asked.

Again, a shake of the head, more determined this time.

"It's been abandoned for years," Jake said. "Evie sold the livestock, but she couldn't bring herself to sell the farm. As far as I know, she never even cleaned it out."

Maggie stared. "Are you saying it hasn't been touched since they died?"

"Well, I certainly couldn't go there." Karen's protest sounded like a pouty young child.

"Maybe you should," Mason said softly.

"Not yet." Jake cleared his throat, a rough, phlegmy sound, and stood. "We need to go back to our house. There are some of your parents' things...of your dad's...that were left to me because we were best friends."

Karen looked startled. "I never knew that!"

A long sigh escaped the old man. "I'm sorry. There's been too much hidden for too long."

Fletcher stood and joined Jake. "Karen may not be too happy about what you have to tell her."

"Yes, but even dirty water is better than rancid mud." He held out his hand to Karen. "Are you ready?"

Karen looked at each of them in turn, then pushed back the quilt and stood. "Let me get dressed."

Karen's silence on the ride to her aunt's house added significantly to the queasy knot in Mason's stomach. Fletcher had bowed out, feeling this needed to be a family discussion without outsiders. But Karen had refused to go without Mason. Jake went ahead in his pickup as Karen got ready. Now Mason drove as Karen stared resolutely out the passenger window of his sports car. Glancing at her occasionally, he wondered exactly how deeply this would wound her.

He tried to imagine how he would feel if he were forced to go back over the day of the fire, the day he watched both of his parents die. After the funerals, he'd left town, never to return. A few years later, he'd sold the farm to a cousin and used the money to pay off his student loans. Closure. A luxury Karen had never had.

Lord, please help her.

The prayer startled him, and he glanced quickly at Karen. *Then again, Lord*—he let the prayer continue—

maybe her influence on me is greater than I realized. He hesitated, then, *Thanks, Lord. I might get the hang of unexpected prayers sooner or later.*

"Turn here." He barely heard her soft words, but when he followed her directions, pulling off the road onto a paved, quarter-mile-long driveway, the queasiness sharpened. The drive followed a curving path up a sloping hill to a massive jigsaw Gothic house that stood out starkly against the bright May sky. Two towers, one at a front corner and the other on the back of the house, dominated the roofline, and the massive front porch stretched around one corner of the house.

"Wow," Mason muttered.

"Yeah, that's what everyone says the first time." Karen snapped the door handle and got out before he'd put the car into Park.

He shifted and opened his door but paused as Karen turned left instead of going to the front porch. Instead, she plunged through thick, calf-high grass around the side of the house to a cluster of outbuildings behind it. Crossing a flagstone patio, she opened the door of the largest one and went in. His curiosity piqued, Mason trailed behind her.

Inside, Jake's pottery studio resembled a larger, older, slightly more cluttered version of Karen's, as if hers had suddenly been supersized. One long wall was filled with ceiling-high shelves, each one loaded with carefully labeled baskets, boxes and plastic containers. Glazes, texturing tools, knives, pattern blocks, brushes and paints sat on worktables as if in constant use. The kilns were larger, but the wheels were about the same size. Jake stood near one, watching. "I knew you'd come here first."

Karen was immovable. "You always knew me best. I thought—" She broke off and looked away a moment, then back at him. "I always felt safe here. I trusted you. I thought you told me everything I needed to know." She motioned around the studio. "About pottery. About life. But you never told me about my own family. You let me pick up everything I know—even about the farm-house!—from people around town. *Why?* Why did you never tell me you and my father were close friends? Why did you never tell me that?"

Jake crossed his arms. "I suppose it would be coy to say that you never asked me."

"Coy. And cruel."

Jake looked her over, taking in the stiff posture, the hard look in her eyes. As he did, he seemed to age a bit. His shoulders dropped forward, and the long sigh he exhaled seemed to deflate him. "We never meant to be cruel, Karen. We just wanted to protect you and keep you safe."

Mason froze a moment, hearing an echo of his father's words, "Hide her and keep her," in Jake's "protect you and keep you safe." *An honest instinct, but is it ever truly possible?*

Karen's voice became even more demanding. "Then tell me, please, that nothing you know could have pre-vented any of this."

Jake pulled two stools from behind a table and motioned for them to sit. Karen perched on the edge of hers, almost as if she were ready to leap up at any second. Mason settled, determined to stay as silent as possible this time.

Jake straddled his own stool. "I'd like to think not, but the truth is, I really don't know."

"That's not helpful."

Jake straightened a bit, then ran his hand through his graying hair. A short, sturdy man in his sixties, Jake's arms and hands still had the firm strength of a lifelong potter, and his voice had the even flow of a man used to dealing with upset women.

"Attitude is not the way to go here, girl. Especially not if you wind up talking with Evie."

"But—"

Jake held up a callused palm. "Just listen for a few minutes." He shifted on the stool and braced his feet flat on the floor, as if preparing for battle. "Your cousin has been pushing us to talk to you for years. Shane cares a lot about you, and he said part of your problems with focus, with relationships, was that you didn't know your history. He said you needed to know your family—all of them—the good, bad and ugly. Evie couldn't do it, though. She still breaks up if she talks too much about Stephanie. That murder tore the entire family apart and just about ripped Evie in half. You may not remember this, but Evie and Stephanie's mother, Elizabeth, died less than two months after. Mrs. Steen had been the center of the family, and Stephanie was its star. Evie was adrift without them."

Karen frowned and closed her eyes. "I remember… I remember a lot of people in the house. Women crying."

Jake nodded. "And she didn't want to, but in some ways, Evie took that out on you."

Karen's eyes opened wide with understanding. "The silences. The outbursts."

"And more. She could barely look at you without thinking of them."

"Then why didn't she send me away?"

He shrugged. "You were still family. Where would you have gone? You stayed with the Elkins a lot, anyway. You and Penny were inseparable. She helped you get through it."

"I stayed there because here was so miserable. At least until you got here."

Jake's craggy face broke into a wry grin. "You were a handful. I think one reason you latched on to me is that you missed your dad more than you understood." He paused, looking slightly over her shoulder and more than twenty years back in time. "You were definitely a daddy's girl. I thought David would burst with pride when you were born."

"How close were you to him?"

Jake brought his gaze back to the present. "We grew up together. He was the athlete, I was the artist. Unlikely friends, but that's what happens in a small town. There were only about twelve boys our age in Mercer. We spent summers together fishing. He taught me to hunt. I taught him to draw well enough to pass art class in school. We didn't go our separate ways until he got that football scholarship at Boston University, while I took an apprenticeship in California. Then he hit the road with your mama, and I went south, to a place in North Carolina where they still dug their own clay out of the riverbanks. Took a while, but we both landed back here."

Karen stood up, stretching her back. "Why would anyone think he had brought his death on himself? That it was his fault?"

Jake rubbed the back of his neck. "The easy answer is that he was a Realtor, and Realtors sometimes make enemies they don't even know they have. But he also had made some strange investments, and the cops wondered where he had gotten the money."

"Where *did* he get the money?"

Jake stood. "Come into the house, both of you. I have some things I want to show you." As they walked, Mason trailing behind, Jake continued the tale. "David, like a lot of New England men, was a stubborn old cuss. He got tired of Mrs. Steen's meddling in his and Stephanie's finances." Jake waved his arm at the side of the house and spoke to Mason. "As you can see, they were raised rich. Mrs. Steen naturally assumed a man who had been raised without much money couldn't possibly manage it. Evie inherited a lot of that attitude. So David set up a front company and started buying, renovating and flipping some of the older homes up near Portsmouth. No one down here knew. The last one he flipped netted him about $150,000. Back in the mid-eighties, that was serious money."

Mason *hmphed.* "Still not exactly petty cash."

Jake chuckled. "No, indeed."

"But flipping isn't illegal or unethical," Mason pressed. "Why would it make someone want to kill him? Did he get involved—" He glanced at Karen and stopped.

Jake knew what he meant, however. "Nope. David wasn't dirty, just private. The cops cleared him and every dime he left behind. Clean, though he may have pushed the limits of ethics. There was some suspicion that David's intense drive to succeed didn't sit well with his competitors. He low-bid them so often that at least one moved his business to Vermont." Jake opened the back door of the house and ushered them into a narrow mudroom, where he slipped off his shoes and motioned for them to do the same. "You've been in my shop and the maid just left. Evie would have a fit."

Karen leaned against a wall to remove her sneakers. "Is she here?"

Jake shook his head. "She left early to run a couple of errands. Then dance class till after noon. We have time."

The mudroom led to an industrial-size kitchen, and Mason fought to keep his mouth from hanging open as they wandered through the house. The dark wood and kitchen scents of smoke, grease and soap gave way to a paneled butler's pantry and a Georgian-style dining room that would seat twenty. Karen, on the other hand, seemed blind to the furnishings as she followed Jake into an elaborate Victorian front parlor, complete with overstuffed horsehair chairs, Tiffany lamps, doilies and the faint aroma of peppermint. On the opposite wall from where they'd entered, a soaring arch opened onto the main entry hall and revealed the curving staircase on the other side.

Jake noticed Mason's slight sniffs of the air and grinned. "Peppermint oil. Supposedly good for the digestion."

Mason wanted to return to the earlier conversation. "No reputable businessman would resort to—"

Jake motioned for them to sit together on one of the Queen Anne sofas. "Business later. Let's switch to the personal now." They both eased down on the cushions, with Mason half expecting the fragile-looking piece to collapse beneath their weight.

Jake opened the front of a secretary and removed a key from a small drawer. He then used it to unlock one of the drawers, from which he withdrew a long, flat wooden box. He placed the box on Karen's lap, nodding at the wooden lid. "Open it."

The box looked as if it had landed in Karen's lap from another century. The inlaid top, with the swirls and distinctive fangs and scales of Chinese dragons, was carved so intricately that it seemed to be almost alive. She ran her fingers over the design. "Amazing."

"Your mother bought it in San Francisco. She kept her prized possessions in there. I brought it here after their deaths. I thought you might want it some day, but Evie wouldn't have it. Said it was too painful for all of us."

Mason stared. "Even after twenty years?"

Jake hesitated, then looked over at him. "Mason, you're young. There are some pains you never quite get over. I hope you never have to learn that from personal experience. Most of us don't, thank God. For Evie, this is one of those wounds."

The lid slid off easily, and Karen carefully placed it beside her on the couch. On top lay a folded piece of yellowed paper. When she opened it, a small "oh" escaped her, and Mason twisted to look over her shoulder.

It was a birth certificate. Not the kind the government issues; this was a hospital certificate with Karen's name, birth details and two tiny footprints. Silently, she handed it to Jake, who nodded. "Yep. Not surprised. They both thought you hung the moon, stars and some of the planets."

Next was a picture featuring a young couple with a baby, surrounded by relatives of every age. Karen showed it to Jake but held on to it. "That's your christening day. I think the whole town turned out. Those are David's folks on his side and Stephanie's on the other."

He pointed to a young woman whose jet-black hair was already streaked with gray, and there was a touch of pride in his voice when he continued.

"That's my Evie. Even though she was a year younger than your mother, she already had Shane. Stephanie and David didn't marry until their mid-twenties, but Evie married Shane's daddy when she was just a kid, barely eighteen. Her mother hated it, hated him, tried her best to stop it. But things were changing during the late sixties, and rebellion was in the air, even in Mercer. He was going off to Vietnam, and he didn't want to lose Evie. Neither of them was old enough to realize he might not come back. Which he didn't."

He pointed to a young boy at Evie's side, who had the same dark hair and blue eyes, and looked about ten years old. "That's Shane there. He came along seven months after his daddy left. David and I did the best we could, but it was hard for him not knowing his father. I suspect that's why he joined the Army early." He paused. "And he wanted Evie to tell you about David."

Jake glanced at Mason. "He knew David and Stephanie pretty well, too, but Karen was only eight or nine when Shane left, so she didn't have him to fill in any blanks, either. They made him a medic, sent him to the Middle East, so he spent more time away."

Mason looked from the picture to Karen's face as she traced the outlines of her mother and father, surprised at the wonder and affection in her face. An awful thought occurred to him. "Don't tell me these are the first pictures you've seen of them!"

Karen barely glanced at him. "Not the first, although

I only have a couple. Pictures of vacations that Mama let me keep."

Mason turned his scowl on Jake, who put up one hand. "I warned you. Evie controls everything where her sister is concerned. She even has most of Karen's inheritance in escrow until she turns thirty, managed by one of the family mutual fund brokers. The Steens are…very private people."

"But this is her family! This is her birthright. How in the world did she get an inheritance put off until Karen turns thirty?"

Karen put a hand on his arm. "Let it go, Mason. It's okay. In a way, Aunt Evie was right. I was always in trouble. I don't know if I could have handled everything when I was a kid. Not sure I can handle it now…." Her words faded as her fingers traced again the figure of her mother, a beautiful young woman with the same narrow face, bright eyes and thick strawberry-gold hair. "We used to laugh about our hair." Her voice turned low and throaty as memories seemed to swirl around her. "We wanted that straight dark hair that Evie had, so lovely and easy to fix. Ours was always tangled and so many clothes clashed with the color. One time…" She paused, smiling shyly. "One time Mama even braided our hair together." She drew a finger from her temple down to the couch to indicate the length of her mom's hair. "Down this side. Thick. We laughed so much that day, trying to keep up with each other. She wound up carrying me half the day so we wouldn't pull our hair out. She said it was a sign we'd never be parted—"

"Jake Abernathy! What are you doing!"

All three of them snapped to their feet, Karen clutching the box to her chest. An enraged Evangeline Abernathy stood in the arched entry from the main hallway, her son, Shane, at her back. Fury had tightened the lines in Evie's face into deep grooves, and her cheeks flared red. "How dare you violate my private space!"

Jake stepped forward, his voice calm. "Evie, you knew it had to happen sooner or later. These belong to Karen. You know Stephanie would want her to have them."

"I know no such—"

"Especially now."

Evie hesitated. "Why now?"

"Her nightmares are back."

Evie's resolve faltered. "You... You should have told me. We should have discussed it."

"You're right. I'm sorry."

Disarmed but still angry, Evie snapped, "Come see me when you're done." She turned on her heels and stomped up the stairs.

Shane shot a thumb's-up at Jake, but shook his head. "Right choice, wrong time, Jake old man."

Jake barely moved. "Shoo," he said simply.

Shane grinned and trotted up the stairs after his mother.

Mason stared after them, disbelieving. The woman who had been so supportive after yesterday's fiasco had come into the room, screamed at her husband and left without even acknowledging that Karen was in the room. No wonder Karen hadn't wanted to come back here when trouble hit.

He turned back to see Jake watching him. The older man cleared his throat. "Not everything is as it seems, Mason."

A dozen responses flitted through Mason's head. He

finally took a deep breath and settled on "I hope so" as the safest.

Jake smothered a laugh as Karen looked at him. Then she sank back down on the sofa with the box in her lap. She pulled out a bundle of letters and photos. "From friends in San Francisco," Jake explained. Two baby teeth in a small drawstring bag. "She felt two made it cute but three was overkill." A lock of Karen's hair and her first report card. Finally, at the bottom, there were two white envelopes, both sealed. As she pulled them out, she looked at Jake, waiting for his explanation.

Her uncle hesitated. "One of these was already in the box. One we found on Stephanie's desk. Evie didn't want anyone to see it."

She opened one and her eyes narrowed in puzzlement at first, then widened in disbelief. "It's to me." Her hands trembled, causing the paper to flutter slightly, as she read.

My darling Karen,
Mother and Evie have been pressuring David and me to get our wills in order, which we've done. But I've decided that you need a legacy of more than money, just in case something happens to your father and me before you're grown.

So I've decided to write a series of letters to you and put them away. If life goes without incident, then you'll be reading this at college, my "good luck with your future, darling" gift, just for you.

If you are, in fact, reading these words at a different time, then I hope you are someplace where you're warm, safe and well cared for. We never meant anything to happen that would hurt you. Your father and I love you more than we thought possible. Someday I hope you have children as beautiful and loving as you are, so you can fully understand our love for the daughter we cherish so much.

As I write this, you are wandering around the house singing "Tomorrow" at the top of your lungs. We're headed for the *Annie* audition in a few days, and you amaze me with your voice and your energy. I hope you get the part.

I also hope that you grow strong, and are a woman worthy of God and all those around you. You leave a bright light among us, everywhere you go, and I hope that light never dims. No matter what anyone says about us, know that we loved you and never did anything unworthy of your love. Trust God, and keep a weather eye on the horizon.

Love,
Mama

By the time she finished, Karen's eyes were bright, her voice tremulous. She folded the letter slowly and slipped it back in the envelope. She licked tears off her lips as she gently returned the envelope to the box. "Now, *this* I needed to hear long ago."

"I'm sorry," Jake whispered.

She nodded, then handed Mason the other envelope. "I can't."

Mason took it. "Are you sure?"

Another nod, and he removed the paper inside. At the top of the page was a note in Stephanie O'Neill's handwriting, but it was brief and to the point. The reply at the bottom was in a more angular, masculine handwriting, and as Mason scanned the words, his stomach tightened into a painful knot. "This we have to take to Fletcher."

Jake and Karen's surprise turned to alarm as he read.

David, I beg you not to go through with this. PLEASE. You have no idea the risk you're taking. This isn't just about money. There is far too much at stake. PLEASE. I love you.
S—
Babe, I understand, but don't worry. I've taken the right precautions. We'll be fine.

Jake leaned back in his chair. "Apparently he did not take enough of the right precautions."

EIGHT

"You realize we haven't really connected what happened to your parents to what's happening now, right? No proof that the face in your dream and on those vases is the one who murdered your parents."

Karen took the letters back from Fletcher and went to stand so close to Mason that their arms touched. "I know. I mean, I've fought the idea for years. It's weird, too much like a bad horror movie idea. But it's just getting…a little odd, don't you think? I mean, obviously Jake thinks there's a connection, and he and Daddy were best friends…." Karen knew she sounded desperate and unsure, but, in a way, she was. The deep sense of frustration, confusion and grief over the events of the past two days had become almost overwhelming. There *had* to be an answer to all this *some*where. Something concrete. "I know it would be easier if I actually recognized the face. I just don't. This isn't just about broken vases. A man *died*, Fletcher. No one kills because he doesn't like a piece of art!"

"No sane person, anyway." Mason's dry voice indicated he thought the killer was crazy, no matter what the reasons.

"So what if I'm sitting on the same kind of information that got my parents killed, without even knowing it?"

Fletcher's gaze went over both of them slowly, then he glanced toward the back wall, and Karen heard a door opening, the one leading to the deck. Finally, he looked back at them and sighed. "Okay. I'll talk to Tyler. We'll go through this again. Maybe this time we'll turn up some ideas of what your father was up to that brought on this trouble. Nothing I've heard from this chat you had with Jake indicates David was doing anything illegal. But maybe more modern research methods will show his legal activities crossed paths with something less legitimate. And, after all, just being legal doesn't mean you don't make enemies. Buying houses to flip them is common around here, so a lot of his business would have been in the public record."

"But not as David O'Neill."

They turned to see Jake entering. "I talked to Evie, and she's agreed to a couple of things." He focused on Karen. "One is to explain more about your father's business, and see if there's any connection that might explain your dreams. Another is to talk to you about your own past, what you've heard around town and what's true."

He pointed behind him. "You know that path from your house to the old Elkins place? Well, it picks up on the other side off their yard and leads directly here. Most folks wouldn't know it because they haven't explored the Elkins backyard."

Fletcher held up both hands. "One thing at a time. Let's start with the business. What do you mean, 'not as David O'Neill'?"

Jake motioned to the sofas. "Let's sit. This may take a while, and I'm getting too old to stand and talk for very long." They settled, and Jake cleared his throat. "David had a front company. If you're going to look for real estate transactions in the mid-eighties, you'll need to search for SDKM Realty Holdings. The first thing you'll probably see is where he mortgaged the farm—literally, in this case—to make his first investments. That's how he got his original capital."

Fletcher took a glass from the tray Maggie carried. "All real estate sales are a matter of public record. Should be easy to find what properties he worked with."

Karen's confusion heightened. "I thought you said this might be about my mother?"

Fletcher nodded. "That's what the crime scene tells me. But I'm the outsider. It's just a theory. We need more info on everything."

Mason slid closer to Karen and touched her arm. "There might be an easier way than stirring up attention by digging through a lot of public records."

"What do you suggest?" Fletcher asked.

Mason turned to Jake. "Did you say that the farm hasn't been touched since they died?"

His eyes brightened. "Indeed it has not."

Mason kept his eyes on Karen. "I don't know about here, but where I come from, most Realtors keep a home office."

"The police probably went through it thoroughly at the time," Fletcher said.

Mason took Karen's hand. "But not with the hindsight of twenty years."

Karen rolled her shoulders back. She didn't know how this could get any more painful, but the tension in all her muscles told her she was in for a rough ride. Yet it had to be done.

Jake cleared his throat. "That's where I come in." When they all turned to look at him, he pointed toward the back of the lodge. "That farm is halfway between the old logging road and the Elkins place." He dug in his pocket and pulled out a heavy key chain. "And I have the key."

Fletcher drove, and his sedan got scraped on all sides by overgrown brush and low-hanging trees. The logging road had been abandoned for many years. Only one home on it remained occupied, and the owner rode a bicycle. About five hundred yards down the road, Jake motioned for Fletcher to stop.

"There used to be a drive that branched off from this road, but it's been overgrown for years, and the path isn't much better. It's not exactly a blazed trail. My guess is that deer and the occasional kid wandering through have kept it as beat down as it is." He focused on Karen. "How are you feeling?"

"Angry," she said softly. "And hurt." She looked about the wooded scene, the blank spots in her memory creating a growing ache in her chest. "I have these tiny memories of Mama and Daddy, and they get further and further away every year." She looked at Mason, suddenly anxious to see how he reacted to her memory loss. "When I woke up in the hospital, I had lost a lot of my memory. I knew who I was and, vaguely, what had happened. I didn't remember where I'd lived… Now I'm thinking Aunt Evie didn't want me to remember, that a clean break with the past was better than a seven-year-old who constantly begged to go home."

Mason tilted his head to one side and a curled lock drooped over his forehead. "Then she was wrong. What she did probably impeded your grieving." Fletcher twisted more in his seat and started to speak, but Mason continued, his tone firm and even but determined. "Yet if there's one thing I've learned from all I went through with my folks, it's that redrawing the past with 'what ifs' is a huge waste of time and mental space."

He reached for her hand, and Karen realized she cherished the warmth and comfort of that simple act. He continued, his voice dropping to a low, quiet baritone. "You need to figure out what happened in your past—not to agonize over what could have been different, but because it's affecting your present."

Karen took a deep breath and squeezed his fingers. "Then let's get started."

The overgrown path made for a rough hike. Twice Karen tripped, grabbing Mason's arm to keep from falling. The day had heated up nicely by the time they reached a wide swatch that looked like a firebreak, choked with weeds, small bushes and saplings but cleared of the older growth trees that shaded the rest of the area. The driveway. They followed the twisting path as it sloped slightly uphill. Karen gripped Mason's hand tighter as they rounded a small copse of trees and the empty farm-house rose before them, like an oasis in a desert.

They stopped, catching their breath, looking over the buildings and yard, all of which were overrun by weeds, wild bushes, briars and trees, as if the forest had tried to regain its lost ground. A barely visible garage had a maple tree pushing up through the roof, and two of the smaller sheds had patches of grass and wildflowers growing on the roof. The gutters on the house had likewise clogged and acquired a collection of blooms and vines that flowed off the roof like trickles of green water.

Karen staggered, her eyelids fluttering. She felt Mason's arm clutch her waist. Flashes of memory seemed to explode in her mind, and she covered her face with her hands. Her mother, glimmering hair flying out behind her, chasing Karen from tree to tree in a frenzied game, both of them giggling wildly, finally collapsing on the grass under…

She straightened, leaning heavily against Mason, and pointed. "That beech. There was a tire swing on that beech." Her breath came in gasps. "Daddy took it down every winter so the rubber wouldn't freeze, and one year he fell…" Her voice trailed away.

Other flashes of memory shot through her mind's eye, tumbling over each other in a tumult of colors, emotions and smells. Images blurred and wavered, as if seen through lace curtains blown about by a breeze. Her mother, singing in the kitchen as she canned fruits and vegetables. Her father, in a backyard workshop. A favorite doll. Dancing for her parents. Singing in the backyard. A puppy. "We had a dog," she murmured, taking a step toward the porch, pointing at the latticework covering the front of it. "He lived under there." More images, some brighter or more violent. Her father cleaning a pistol. A child's view from the top of the stairs of a shouting match between her parents. No, not her parents. Her mother and…someone wearing bright green.

She staggered again, letting Mason support much of her weight, which he did with reassuring strength. The dizziness caused by the swirl of conflicting memories threatened to overwhelm her, and a sense of panic gripped her. "Why is this happening to me?" she whispered, startled at the sound of desperation in her voice.

Fletcher took her other arm. "Repressed memories can be overpowering, and sometimes it doesn't take much to trigger them."

Karen pushed away from them and went to the porch, barely hearing Jake's words of caution. "Careful. That porch has been rotting for twenty years."

She nodded, picking her footing carefully as she climbed the steps. "I have to go in. I have to."

No one stopped her. The thick planks under her feet creaked and bowed under her weight, but they held. When she got to the door, she turned, and Jake tossed her the key. The rusty lock protested but opened. The door needed more encouragement, after swelling and contracting through winters past. Karen stepped inside…and sneezed. As she pinched her nose and upper lip to prevent more, she felt Mason behind her.

He touched her arm. "Are you okay, *chère?*"

She nodded. "Jake wasn't kidding about nothing being touched."

He peered around her, a sputtering of French bursting from under his breath.

Karen knew how he felt. In front of them lay a tableau of three lives frozen in time. A heavy film of greasy dust and spider webs coated everything, and leaves blown in through the broken windows lay scattered about, but in spite of it all, the scene could have been lifted from any living room from the 1980s.

An open paperback book, now yellow and brittle, lay pages down on the couch. Near it, a quilted throw was draped as if someone had just thrown it back and gotten up although the colors were now faded and dull. A nearby desk held an ancient Kaypro computer, a stack of floppy disks and a scattering of bills waiting to be paid. An early Atari game system was hooked up to a television near the couch. "I used to play that," Karen said, her voice drifting into the past. "Daddy wanted us to stay up to date on everything." Paint on the walls had peeled off in great hunks, and the ceiling showed signs of water damage, but Karen was lost in her memories and noticed.

She went to the couch and looked down at the book. A much-read Georgette Heyer. "Mama read romances all the time. Daddy used to tease her about wanting him to be more handsome, and I used to insist that wasn't possible."

The scramble of visions in her brain started to settle, achieving a bit of coherence. She looked around at Mason, then Fletcher and Jake, who'd followed them inside unnoticed. She took a deep breath. "Daddy's office is upstairs."

The broad, dark wood steps of the staircase felt surprisingly sturdy as they all climbed to the second floor. Karen paused to stroke the banister, which stood firm despite the lack of heat and air-conditioning in the house. "My grandfather was a carpenter. He thought he was building this house to last a lifetime." She paused and looked around at them again. "I don't know how I knew that."

Fletcher pressed his finger against his upper lip, apparently trying not to break into a fit of sneezing. "My guess is that little bits like that will increasingly come back to you as everything slips back into place. Most kids have memories dating back to when they were three and four. Yours have just been held hostage."

Karen's sense of panic had begun to ease. "I think

you may be right." She paused. "This may sound really odd, but…this is beginning to feel like home."

"Not odd at all." Mason smiled warmly. "This *is* your home. Your birthright."

Taking a deep breath—and fighting another sneeze—she pointed to her right. "The office should be in there." She stepped inside the room and stopped, grinning suddenly. "And here's Lisa."

"What?" Fletcher's startled question caused Mason and Jake to step aside.

Karen chuckled and pointed to her father's desk, and the chunky-looking computer that sat on one side. "That's a Lisa. One of the first Apple computers. Didn't stay on the market long. I told you, Daddy wanted all the newest gadgets. His workshop out back is full of…" Her voice trailed off again, and she looked at Fletcher. "Will I ever get used to this?"

Fletcher shook his head. "Not for a while. You're a smart woman, you were probably just as smart as a kid. I'm sure you took in everything, storing more than you realized."

A sense of wonder and comfort settled over her. "I just can't believe it. All this time…" She set her shoulders, determined now to find all the answers, no matter what. "My father was a woodworker. It was one reason he loved old houses."

Fletcher grinned. "Okay. Let's see what we can find."

Mason turned to Fletcher. "If that computer didn't crash and hasn't been turned on in twenty years, do you think the tech guys in New York could get anything off the hard drive?"

The tall detective shrugged. "Probably not, but it

never hurts to ask." He went to the desk and opened the top drawer. Inside, Karen could see a brown accordion-style folder held shut by age and rubber bands that had long ago dry-rotted. "Good a place as any to start." Fletcher carefully lifted it out, ignoring the rubber bands that dropped away in pieces. Gently, he opened the folder and slid the papers that were inside onto the desk.

In a house that had experienced frigid temperatures in the winter and scorching summer heat, the papers had turned yellow and brittle. As he tried to separate the folded sheets, many simply broke apart in his hands. As he continued, barely breathing over the fragile pieces, Jake continued the search of the desk, while Mason began prowling through a closet.

Karen, however, felt herself drawn to a tall, narrow bookcase near the door. Her memories continued to unfold in her head, but the feeling wasn't quite as unsettling as before. She had grown curious, however, to see what would pop up next, almost as if she'd opened a book in the middle and was trying to figure out the plot and characters.

Books. Her parents had loved books. On the bottom shelf of this case were her father's real estate books, sales training manuals, books on property laws. But the other shelves were clustered with her mother's beloved romances and her father's fascinating Christian fantasies. C. S. Lewis and J. R. R. Tolkien were still propped against Jane Austen and Janette Oke. They had both loved Dorothy Dunnett's Lymond Chronicles. She paused at that… Her father had loved Dunnett. He'd read some of the books to her, holding her spellbound for hours. There, on his top shelf, was a hardback copy of *Checkmate.*

This, sweet pea, is the book that changed my life. You're too young, but when you're old enough, we'll share it.

"Oh, Daddy." She reached for the book, opening it slowly. A special edition on acid-free paper, the dust jacket proclaimed. The cover and pages were still in excellent condition, barely cracking as she turned a few pages. As she did, a slip of paper fluttered to the floor. She picked it up, holding it flat in her palm.

R10 L23 R45

She took it to Fletcher, excitement tightening her chest. "Is this what I think it is?"

He paused and looked at the paper. "If you think it's a combination to a lock, you're probably right."

Jake looked around at them. "What kind of lock?"

"How about a safe?"

They turned to stare at Mason, who had shoved aside the clothes in the closet and pried away a loose panel in the back. Behind it, mounted firmly in the wall, was a black fireproof safe. Easily measuring two feet square, it looked as shiny and new as the day it had been installed.

Fletcher nodded at Karen. "Give it a try."

She rushed to the safe and dropped to her knees. The dial on the safe spun easily, and she twisted through the combination, her fingers trembling. She said a quick prayer, then clutched the handle. It turned without hesitation, and she pulled open the door.

Unlike the papers in the desk, the ones in the black box were pristine and flexible. A thick stack of double-folded legal papers on one side appeared to be mortgages, and Karen pulled them out, along with an old-fashioned blue ledger, passing them to Fletcher. There were a few miscellaneous-looking papers underneath, and Mason took those, gathering them slowly and taking them to the desk. Only a large cardboard box remained, and Karen tugged it toward the front, surprised by its weight. Remembering the memory treasures in her mother's Chinese dragon box, Karen eased the box to the floor and eagerly opened it.

And froze.

She was still staring into the box when Fletcher cleared his throat and sniffed. "Well, I think I've found some of the source of animosity between David O'Neill and Evangeline Steen Abernathy." He had their attention as he held up a legal-looking document. "This is the deed to the Steen family estate, purchased by SDKM Realty Holdings. David O'Neill bought Evie's home."

"There's more," Mason said quietly. "In this stack is a letter of intent to sell the adjacent property, and a letter from a builder willing to develop the property, provided the price was right."

"I think," Karen said evenly, trying to ignore the numbness growing in her legs and stomach, "that the price must have been right."

The three men gathered around her, looking down. Bank-wrapped bundles of twenty-dollar bills filled the box in front of her.

"Bingo," muttered Fletcher.

"This is getting sorely out of hand." Eyes narrowed to slits, Luke's client watched the old farmhouse. The pottery supplies Karen had carried with her from the house had been deposited in the retreat studio, so keeping an eye on her had become a necessary tactic to ensure she didn't make any more face vases. Her pottery had never been the real issues; just those vases. She could do any other kind of pottery she possibly conceived of in that unimaginative little mind of hers, but those faces had to go away before someone noticed. Someone *else*. Before someone *else* saw what was really coming out of Karen O'Neill's demented soul.

"My face." Fingers pressed to the upper lip of that face trembled. "Don't make me do anything worse. Please."

Obviously Karen's memory had started to return. The way she had pranced around the yard, moving immediately to the tree where that dangerous swing had been, pointing to the hole in the latticework where that wretched dog the O'Neills had kept so long had wormed his way under the porch. Not a good sign at all. Once she started remembering even the smallest things about her parents… No. Not good.

The client grew still, camouflaged by the shadows, as Karen, Mason and Fletcher emerged from the house. Mason, as weak and protective as ever, tried to comfort an obviously shaken Karen. He carried a stack of folded legal papers and a ledger tucked under one arm, while Fletcher lugged an obviously heavy box, his biceps and forearms straining with the effort.

"No! They can't have!" The hoarse whisper burst from the client, who clamped a mouth tight and backed into the undergrowth. All these years, searching for the combination! Tears stung the corners of pale eyes, which narrowed.

Wait. Where was that overgrown boy of a potter?

The first three had almost gotten to the path when they

paused and turned. After a moment Jake appeared, carrying a wooden tray bearing the computer from David O'Neill's office. The four disappeared down the path.

Waiting until they were well out of sight and hearing, the client broke from the undergrowth and dashed across the overgrown yard. Feet long accustomed to the frail porch quickly crossed the safest boards and padded up the wooden staircase. Dust on the desk had been scattered hither and yon, and a bare spot remained where the Lisa had sat. Fools. It couldn't possibly work after all those years in the heat and cold. But there, *there,* in the office closet, the safe stood open.

Anguish shot through the client, who sank to the floor, fists clenched. So it was true after all. Despite all her denials, all Stephanie O'Neill's claims turned out to be hollow. There had been a hidden stash of money, money carefully guarded against Elizabeth Steen's prying, against David O'Neill's risky ventures. She *had* been lying!

A smile spread slowly across the client's face. Her death had been justified after all.

The satisfaction suddenly vanished. Once Karen went through those papers, once she understood what they meant, she might remember it all, including the owner of that face. Now they were both on a path with only one destination.

Slowly that brief satisfaction gave way to anger, then to a cold, determined sense of numbness. The fear had to stop clouding every night. The pain had to cease.

Only one choice.

NINE

The ride back to the retreat remained quiet and somber, with each of them lost in their own ponderings about the findings at the old farmhouse. Karen curled up in a corner of the backseat, staring out the window—and into some distant time and place.

Mason couldn't imagine how it must feel to rediscover all those wonderful little memories about your parents, only to find out, moments later, that they may not have been who you thought they were.

Once they were at the retreat, Karen got out of the car and went immediately into her bedroom and locked the door. When Mason started to follow her, Fletcher stopped him. "Let her be," he said, so low that no one else could hear. "Sometimes women just have to cry it out."

The thought made Mason's chest ache, but he inhaled deeply, steeling his nerves, and asked if he could do anything to help.

"No. I'm going to take the computer and the money into Boston, talk to some friends of mine. One's a retired forensic tech with the NYPD computer department. If anyone can reboot that computer, he can. I'll get the money checked, as well."

Jake gave Maggie the legal documents for her opinion, then took a hike around the property to work off his anxiety and to wait for Karen to awaken. So the afternoon's activities were set—for everyone but Mason. As the house grew still, he walked out on the back deck and leaned on the rail, looking out over the glorious view.

The lodge house sat halfway down a long, sloping granite hillside. While the front lawn dropped gracefully from the road to the main entrance, the back deck overlooked the bottom half of a valley filled with trees, wildflowers and brush. The ten cabins of the retreat were scattered over that piece of woodland, slowly disappearing from view as the trees reached full leaf and the vibrant dappled colors of the flowers vanished behind the thick undergrowth. Come fall, the valley would turn into a supreme example of God's autumn handiwork. Maggie once told him she felt this view was one of the finest in all New England. "Finestkind," she'd said with a wry grin.

It was truly a grand place to live, to write, to create. When Aaron Jackson had planned this place as his legacy, he'd intended it to be an oasis of respite, not the location for some of the most turbulent times of any artist's life. Mason wondered if Karen would ever be able to find peace about what had happened. "Especially," he said aloud, "when we've only scratched the surface."

He walked to the deck steps and sat, his elbows on his knees. Around him, a light wind stirred the trees, causing the beech and maples to rustle and the pines to whisper lightly. He closed his eyes, letting his mind drift back over his own childhood, over long evenings with his father on the porch of their home, listening to the pines and cypress, waiting for his mother to come home from yet another one of her trips. It was one of his favorite memories, even though his mother was not a part of it.

His father always lit a pipe, blowing the smoke around them to keep away the mosquitoes, while Mason sat on the porch floor doing his homework. They did this often, both of them preferring to be outside rather than cooped up in the house. This time, however, Mason, at sixteen, had begun to question his mother's long absences. He stared out across their yard and down the drive. His father cleared his throat and spoke in that rough way of his, almost as if reading his son's thoughts.

"Your mother, she's a good woman. She's just got something here—" he tapped his chest "—that makes her want to go. Wander. Go see other places, other countries. We love only each other, though. You know that, don't you, boy?"

Mason fought the heat in his face, not wanting to admit even to himself what he'd been thinking. "Papa, that's not—"

His father waved the pipe. "I was young. I know you see her leave. I know you see your friends with their parents getting divorced all the time. I'm old, not blind." He paused, taking a deep pull on the pipe. "But this thing she has in her soul, this is not about us. I know her. She does not go with other men. I don't go with other women. What we have, it comes along only once in a life, and we both know that. She would die for me. I would die for her."

At the time, the teenaged son thought his father was

indulging in a bit of romantic hyperbole. Mason now knew all too well how true that was. A year later, his father had, in fact, died for the woman he'd loved so dearly.

Can I be that kind of man? Problem was, he had too much of his mother in him, as well. As deeply as his feelings ran for Karen, he also felt the pull of the horizon, almost constantly. Even now he wanted both to leave her alone and give her space, as well as take her in his arms, vowing never to leave her. "And I thought Karen was the confused one here," he muttered.

Mason closed his eyes. *If it works for Karen...* "Lord," he whispered. "I'm not good at this, but we could use Your help." He paused. "*I* could use Your help."

He sat there for a bit, eyes closed, feeling the wind and listening to the swaying trees. Hundreds of images fluttered through his mind, from his mother and father sharing a moment of tenderness to Karen's vases to the feel of the clay under his fingers to a painful vision of the flames that had consumed his own childhood home...

So I went down to the potter's house, and I saw him working at the wheel. But the pot he was shaping from the clay was marred in his hands; so the potter formed it into another pot, shaping it as seemed best to him.

Mason's eyes snapped open. It was the verse Karen had quoted to him yesterday. "So we're still works in progress, right, Lord?"

He smiled and straightened a bit, then jumped as a voice came from behind him.

"Praying?" Maggie asked.

Mason started to stand, but she waved him to stay put and sat beside him, handing him a sandwich wrapped in a napkin. "I can understand. I do a lot of it myself. I'd go crazy if I didn't."

"Karen does it all the time. Seemed like it might be worth the effort." He peered at the sandwich's contents, then ate quickly, suddenly realizing how hungry he was.

Maggie remained silent a few moments, looking out over the landscape. "I'm about to get personal with you, Mason, but it's important."

"Okay."

"I can't help notice you get this sort of lost-puppy look when you're around Karen. How well do you know her?"

Mason's cheeks burned. "Lost puppy?"

Maggie grinned. "Kind of like you could swallow her whole without a whole lot of effort. It's very becoming on you."

The young professor returned the grin. "Thanks. I think." He tilted his head to look more closely at her. "I know her about as well as two people could after only a few months. Why?"

Maggie took a deep breath and straightened her back. "David and Stephanie O'Neill have always been seen as martyrs around here. Smart, sweet young couple, just doing their best. Because of their hippie days, few folks ever thought of them as anything else. A little wild, but small-town naive. No one, and I mean *no one,* would have ever conceived of David as a ruthless businessman."

"But apparently he was."

She nodded. "But no one saw it that way. After all, the police never found any business-related reason for the crime. All these years, folks have thought it was a random act. A crime of opportunity. Because of the horrid way they'd died, Karen has been colored by that her whole life. Victim. When Evie turned out to be, well, not exactly the most loving of mother substitutes, her church, the whole town, in fact, adopted Karen. The older people around here, especially at her church, they all see her as something like their own daughter or granddaughter. Now, with all this going on, sympathies are running even higher."

"You think that's about to change."

Maggie shrugged. "It could for some. It's about to get personal and nasty, and I suspect the violence against Karen will probably escalate."

Mason glanced quickly at the house, as if to see through the walls into Karen's room. Maggie patted his arm. "She's okay. I just checked. Took her a sandwich, too. But I also called Tyler, and he's on his way back over."

"You found out a lot of stuff?"

"More than you can imagine. Remember that I have to do a lot of background checks on people before they come here, so we pay to maintain access to a few databases that the public doesn't have access to. Also, as the head of the retreat's foundation board, I work with our accountant on our taxes and the real estate investments. Jake will probably be able to provide more specifics later about some private items. However, most of what I found out online is a matter of public record. The difference between David's personal records and what I can access now is that twenty years ago, the Internet was still an infant learning to roll over in its crib. Now it can fly."

A horn sounded from the front of the house, and Maggie stood up. "That's Tyler. Get Karen and meet me in my office. Bring Jake if he shows back up."

Karen answered his faint knock on her door, but, unlike Fletcher had predicted, she showed no signs of having shed any tears. In fact, the look on her face showed more determination than grief, with her mouth a thin line and eyes bright and clear. He followed her to Maggie's office, just as Jake returned and joined them. Converted from a bedroom and located in the opposite wing of the lodge, Maggie's office was Spartan and practical. Karen and Tyler sat in the chairs in front of Maggie's desk, while Mason stood near the door, observing.

Maggie sat and placed her hands flat on two of the documents. "How much do you know about back taxes?"

Karen frowned and they all shook their heads. "Not much," Tyler said.

Releasing a long breath, Maggie plunged right in. "David O'Neill knew a lot. In fact, one of his gifts seemed to be locating properties that were in trouble because of either unpaid property taxes or mortgage payments. I'm not sure why he set up a separation between the real estate work he did as David O'Neill and the property acquisition and refits he did as SDKM Realty Holdings, but he did. I can draw some conclusions from the facts, but they'll be assumptions about someone I never met."

"Make them," said Tyler bluntly.

Maggie's chin dropped a bit, and she glanced at all four quickly before continuing. Mason shifted positions so he could better watch Karen's face, which seemed unusually reserved.

"As David O'Neill, he conducted basic real estate transactions here in Mercer and in the surrounding areas. Nothing out of the ordinary for a one-man agency. The SDKM properties were mostly around Portsmouth or Boston, and primarily constituted foreclosure properties in historic districts that he 'flipped.' That is, he bought them way under market, renovated them, then sold for a substantial profit."

Mason cleared his throat. "Given what Jake said about Evie and her mother meddling in his financial affairs, he may have wanted to keep the more lucrative areas of his business quiet and out of their reach."

"No doubt," Jake muttered. "Mrs. Steen regularly dug into the business of everyone in the family. Evie has cousins who still won't talk to her."

Maggie nodded at him. "My thoughts exactly."

Tyler shifted uncomfortably. "But real estate transactions are a matter of public record. How did he keep these quiet?"

Maggie's gaze moved to Karen. "Because SDKM Realty Holdings wasn't registered to David. It was registered to Karen."

Karen remained still, which increased Mason's sense of worry tenfold. In fact, she barely blinked at Maggie's revelation, a fact that seemed to bother Maggie, as well. The retreat manager looked down a moment, as if to check her facts.

"That's why they didn't find the company twenty years ago. They looked only for connections under David's name."

Tyler looked puzzled. "So Karen inherited SDKM?"

"Yes and no." Maggie grimaced. "Technically, she

already owned it, so there was nothing to inherit. David set it up similar to the way income for child stars is handled. Profit for the corporation went into an endowment fund that would be available to Karen when she turned eighteen." She tapped the blue ledger. "The corporation took out only basic operating expenses."

Jake crossed his arms. "David had a lot of smarts and more than a little suspicion of his in-laws. He once told me that SDKM was created for Karen so that she could have an income independent of the family, and wouldn't be dependent on their whims if she wanted to choose a college or pursue a career outside their approval." He looked at Karen. "Your grandmother could be extremely domineering, and Stephanie was definitely her favorite child. David could see what that had done to Evie and Stephanie both. Mrs. Steen never forgave Evie for marrying a soldier, then having Shane without a husband, even one Mrs. Steen despised. She didn't realize that Evie was more like her than Stephanie ever thought about being. Your father didn't want that kind of family drama and power to run your life like it did Stephanie and Evie's."

Mason shifted his weight from one foot to the other. "So who inherited the control of SDKM?"

Maggie shifted a few papers around. "That's where it gets sticky. These are copies of their wills. They show that Stephanie's will left everything to David, then Karen. David's did the same in reverse—Stephanie, then Karen, including SDKM. Guardianship of Karen, in the event she was still a minor, went to Evie."

Shaking his head, Jake looked at the floor, his eyes distant. "You can't imagine the reaction when that came out. The shock that went through the family when the wills were probated was life-altering. Until then, none of them had known anything about SDKM or Evie's guardianship. Mrs. Steen was so mortified, family legend has it that the knowledge killed her."

Maggie leaned back in her chair before continuing to her silent audience. "But that wasn't true, was it?"

He shook his head, then looked up at Karen. "Your grandmother had ovarian cancer. She ignored the symptoms until it was too late. The docs found it a few months before David and Stephanie were murdered, but Elizabeth refused treatment near the end."

"So Evie got everything from everybody?" Tyler asked.

Maggie held up a finger. "Wait. It gets better. When Karen was sixteen, Evie took her doctor's and school records and requested a court evaluation, claiming that Karen would never be responsible enough at eighteen to inherit her parents' bequests. She asked that everything be put on hold until Karen turned thirty-five. That maybe by then Karen would have a real career. The judge made it thirty instead."

A small boil of anger stirred in Mason's gut. "But as executrix of the wills, that left Evie in charge of all funds."

"Right," Maggie responded, "She couldn't use them except for Karen's welfare and management of the estate, but she did have charge of them for investment purposes." She faced Karen again. "I found nothing to imply Evie is doing anything that's not what she thinks is in your best interest."

Jake seemed to come to life again. "Now, wait a minute—"

Mason pressed on. "But it makes for a good motive

if something happens to Karen. Evie's her next of kin."
Before anyone could respond, he turned to Karen. "Did
you know any of this?"

Karen blinked up at him as if waking from a dream.
"Of course, I knew Evie had asked for the delay of the
inheritance. I was in court when it happened. I begged
to receive it when I was twenty-five, but she wouldn't
relent. I didn't know what all was involved." She looked
pointedly at Jake. "But I didn't know a lot that I should
have until today. I'd never heard anything about SDKM
until this morning."

Jake shifted his weight. "Karen, child—"

"I can understand that," Tyler muttered. At their
surprised looks, he straightened, speaking more
clearly to Karen. "Think about it from Evie's point of
view. You couldn't remember much about your parents, not the farmhouse, nothing. Around here, they're
thought of as the hippie kids who did okay, but not
great. If you think you're asking for extra money for
pottery supplies, you're not going to try as hard as you
might have if you thought you'd be inheriting
millions." He shrugged. "She's not going to mention
a corporation in your name you could already legiti-
mately control."

Maggie's voice darkened. "Evie's not her only family, Tyler. You talk about her as if she has the only motive
for the murders."

"Evie didn't kill anyone!" Jake's face reddened.
"She's not perfect, but this is my wife!"

Silence fell, and Tyler turned to Mason. Clearly,
Mason realized, they were thinking the same thing.

Karen looked at the floor. "Jake's right. She raised

me. She loves me. She may be a little cold, but she's not a monster."

"True," Maggie said firmly. "And she's not the only one with a motive. This goes way beyond family." She definitely had their attention as she dug through a stack of the paperwork, pulling out three sheets of expensive-looking letterhead. One had a yellow sticky note on it. "These letters were tucked in the ledger, near the back. They're from a man named Carver Billings."

Karen sat upright. "Who?"

Maggie glanced at her computer screen. "Carver Billings. He ran a construction company in the seventies and eighties. Based in Boston but with branches in Portsmouth and Providence. From all that I can find, he competed with David for several properties, including a major historic renovation in Providence worth more than a million. David got the contract. These letters are from Billings, threatening David with a lawsuit and possible investigation, claiming that the only way David could bid so low would be if he were corrupt." She pointed to the yellow slip. "David's note here is a reminder to call his lawyer." She dropped the papers on the desk. "It all became moot. David's murder caused a default, and Billings picked up the job."

"That's not all he picked up." Karen's eyes shone and a new determination strengthened her voice. "Evie told me yesterday. Shane sold Carver Billings the Elkins estate."

Frustrating woman! After the morning farmhouse visit, Karen had disappeared into that rabbit warren of a retreat, not to be seen again. The client had spotted her moving around the lodge at one point, but nothing since.

Given the maze of trails in the woods of the retreat, there was no telling which direction she'd wandered in. Or if she still hid out in the lodge.

He'd seen the police chief and that writer boy leave and head into town, each looking as if he'd swallowed a toad. *Good! They deserve a little unhappiness in life. Get used to it.*

Karen, however, had not been with them, and the last time Maggie had walked in front of those glass walls, she'd been alone. Perhaps Karen had gone to the studio to work…not good. But neither was the idea that Karen would ramble about the woods or go back to the farmhouse.

Well…if I can't go to her, then she'll have to come to me. A dozen different ideas came to mind, each one guaranteed to pull Karen O'Neill out of hiding. But one in particular stood out.

A slow smile pulled at the corners of the client's mouth. "Do not toy with me, girl. You are not adequate in this game. Not skilled at all."

No need to wait and watch. Dusk would be descending soon, and a few purchases were needed before Karen could be smoked out. The client turned toward Mercer, indulging in a low chuckle at the thought.

TEN

An inexplicable desire to run away overwhelmed Karen as Maggie and Tyler both began peppering her with questions about Shane's sale. *Too much, it's all too much.* She stood, her desire becoming a craving that drove all other thoughts out of her head. She put up her hands, as if to ward off any more questions, blurting out the only thing that came to mind.

"I need my clay!"

The room fell silent, and, head down, Karen brushed by Mason. Her hands almost itched, and her fingers curled repeatedly around an invisible lump of earth as she headed toward the back door. She needed to work.

Behind her the chatter started again, but no one followed her. Good. Truly good. She needed her solitude and her clay.

And her God.

Tears stung her eyes as she descended the steps of the lodge's back deck and headed for the studio. Her muttered prayer for help, guidance and—*please!*—wisdom felt rapid-fire, desperate and confused. But God would know. God always knew.

Karen yanked the studio door open. A broad, airy space, it still smelled like freshly cut wood and paint. White, noontime light showered the room. Canvases were stacked in one corner, and her pottery supplies and clay rested on a table near a set of large windows.

Sterile. It was the first word that came to mind. Too clean. Definitely not where she wanted to work. "No, no, no," she muttered, turning and closing the door again. "I want to go home." She paused, then spotted the trail head, knowing all too well that it led to the logging road, then past her farm—

My farm.

—then past the Elkins place, over Oak Drive and past Evie's, ending, finally, at her own home, the cottage with the tall windows and the perfect studio. It had been years since she'd walked even a partial length of the trail, but it would give her the time she needed away from all this. Breaking into a trot, she hit the trail and disappeared beneath the shelter limbs and broad leaves of the deep New England woodland.

From the lodge house deck, Jake and Mason watched Karen disappear into the woods.

"Not good. Not good at all. She shouldn't wander off by herself like this."

Mason agreed. "I'm going—" He broke off as Jake grabbed his arm.

"No. Let me. I know where she's going. She needs answers." The old man inhaled deeply, looking ten years older. "She deserves answers."

Mason had no sympathy. "Long overdue answers."

Jake nodded, then headed down the steps. Mason

watched as he disappeared down the same path as Karen.

"Lord," he said aloud. "Watch them."

After a quarter mile or so, Karen slowed her pace, inhaling deep gulps of the fresh air. Her eyes still burned from tears, but she brushed them away, knowing these were more from the exercise and the wind than emotions. Still…anxiety and confusion gripped her heart. The overload of information, the rush of forgotten memories were numbing her mind and draining her energy. She felt lost, as if she'd forgotten how to form even reasonable thoughts. In the past thirty-six hours, she'd taken in so much that none of it made sense anymore.

"Lord," she mumbled, finding an even pace for the trail, "I need a break. And a whole lotta help."

As she walked, her body moved easily into a familiar rhythm, one that had developed as she'd grown up exploring the hiking trails, woods and lakes of New Hampshire. As she walked, her thoughts drifted to those times, seeking refuge in things she actually did remember well, things she cherished. Long summer days with Penny, rambling in the parks, turning empty swing sets into alpine chateaux, trees into castles and seesaws into Amelia Earhart's plane. Penny's china doll collection became an audience for their plays, and sometimes Mrs. Elkins would open up the attic, which was a treasure trove of grown-up clothes, hats, exotic furniture and—

Karen tripped, preventing a fall by catching the trunk of a young tree. Her shoulder smacked a low branch, and a sharp pain shook the left side of her body. "Yow!"

She pushed back away from the tree, rubbing her upper arm. "Man, that's gonna leave a mark." The remark made her giggle, and she leaned against the tree, letting a good old-fashioned fit of laughter wash over her. Karen slid to the ground, relishing the moment.

Finally, the giggles subsided and she let out a long sigh as much of her tension and anxiety leeched away with the laughter. "I guess, Lord," she said, looking up at the sun through the leaves, "a little hysteria never hurt anyone."

A brisk wind stirred the trees around her, pushing her hair away from her face. Karen closed her eyes and tilted her head back, letting the heat of the sun and the twists of the breeze wash over her. "Lord, I so need Your direction. I'm scared and I can make sense of none of this. Why is this happening now?"

The calming sounds of the forest surrounded her. The rustle of the leaves nearby as a squirrel searched for food. Birdsongs bounced from branch to branch. Somewhere in the distance, a dog called for his master. The swirls of air through tree limbs and underbrush were like a whispered calling song, each echoing the other as the breeze passed through.

"Because it needed to."

The answer was her own. Maybe. Yet, somewhere in the back of her mind, she knew that her parents' final tale had to come out, sooner or later. And what better time than when she had the support of Fletcher, Maggie, Jake and Tyler? And Mason.

Mason. The flash of his dark eyes made her breath catch. And the way he'd hovered the last thirty-six hours…as if he wanted to take care of her but wasn't sure if he should. In other men it would have made her feel smothered, but there had been moments when she'd just wanted to collapse against him and take comfort in his arms.

"Some independent woman you are," she scoffed at herself, then immediately reflected on her thoughts about the timing of all this, that it'd happened just when she did have the right support.

"It's all so confusing, Lord. Help me find my way." With a sigh, she stood up and resumed her hike, more determined than before. Instead of dwelling on details, however, Karen let her mind drift, and it tumbled rapidly between old memories and new, thoughts of Penny and play, Jake and clay and the flashed glimpses of her mother and father that seemed to be growing stronger, clearer, as the hours passed.

What grew even stronger than her memories, however, was the sense of the love and affection her parents had had for her—and she for them. What had begun as a flickering image of her mother chasing her around the yard had fleshed out with smells of newly mown grass, wild onions and the scent of her mother's perfume. Karen found herself remembering the warmth and comfort of her mother's hugs and the strength of her father's shoulders as he'd lifted her.

"How could I have forgotten those, Lord? Will the memories help me through this?"

As her mind roamed the past, her steps brought her to the logging road, and she stopped. The gravel road, overgrown but still visible, had once been the access to a large tree farm as well as the driveway to her parents' place. Now it led only to one small cottage, not yet visible from this spot where the trail crossed. The farm driveway, however, lay only a few yards up, and Karen could see the indentation in the road's edge that marked it.

"No." Her voice sounded flat. "I want to go home." She turned to the trail opening directly across from her, and guided her steps toward it.

What is home?

Karen stopped in the middle of the road, the thought making her throat constrict. Evie's house wasn't, even though she'd grown up there. She had no desire to ever live there again. Even with Jake there, its sterility and darkness felt oppressive. The Elkins' place had come closer, but still…it wasn't hers. Her own tiny house shone in her mind, and she thought about how hard she'd worked to make it her nest, her warm, comforting refuge. Definitely a home, but hers as an adult. Where did her childhood belong?

The farm, which she'd known about less than a day, tugged at her. Or maybe she tugged at it. "I give in," she muttered. "I want more." She headed up the road, her steps retracing those of that morning as she picked her way over the drive, pausing at the edge of the weed-choked yard. Had it really only been a few hours ago?

The jumble in her brain felt as if it had been building for a lifetime…and perhaps it had. She'd retreated to her room when they'd returned to the lodge in an effort to let her mind adjust—to separate the flood of re-pressed memories from what she'd had prior, but to no avail. Now…

Karen let her gaze travel slowly from the house, to the barn behind it, to a third building *(Daddy's work-*

shop?) on the far side of the barn. Two smaller structures struck her as being a chicken coop (*we awoke to roosters crowing!*) and corn crib (*Mama hated the mice that lived there*). The small memories amazed Karen now—how bread had smelled or that the sun had risen over those trees—instead of the more eventful ones from earlier. They were the true signs that she had lived there; this had been her home.

The rush of images that had overwhelmed her earlier began to slow as she crossed the yard toward the workshop. She didn't want to return to the house just yet. Instead, there was something about this smaller building that spoke to her. The door was latched but not locked, and she pulled it open. The hinges protested with a hardy squawk but gave way and opened with a rough, grainy feel. Karen stepped inside the door and back in time twenty years.

It had been a Saturday. Her father had been working on a new table for the dining room, turning the legs on his lathe, sweat soaking his Jimmy Buffett T-shirt and rolling down his temples and cheeks. Yet he'd smiled through the work, a look of joy on his face. Karen had been there, playing among the shavings, making letters out of the longer curls, like a giant, splintery alphabet soup. Her mother had come in, bringing them both lemonade. They had laughed, and Karen had broken into her audition song for the next day.

Karen snapped back to the present. The next day, they had died. "No wonder I wanted to come in here."

The workshop had not been touched, except by time and weather. A thick layer of dust covered everything, and long strands of spider webs dangled from the rafters and windowsills. A heavy, musty smell permeated the air, made up of moldy earth, damp wood and machine oil. Two of the windows had cracked. The last leg of the table was still secured in the lathe, although it had bowed, cracked and turned gray with age. Other tools, including her father's beloved collection of wooden hand planers, were just as he'd left them that Saturday night, when he'd returned to the house.

She reached out, her hand gently touching the table leg. "Amazing no one stole them," Karen muttered.

"No one knew they were here."

Yelping, Karen spun, her hand to her throat. Jake straightened, fighting a smile. "Sorry. Thought you'd heard me."

Karen caught her breath. "No. I think I was lost in time. What are you doing here?"

"I followed you. I wondered if you'd come back after this morning."

Karen looked around. "It called me back."

"No doubt. Feeling overwhelmed?"

Karen faced him. "I feel like I've had another person move into my head. A little girl who has all these memories that I should have grown up with—but didn't. Why did no one ever tell me?"

Jake clasped his hands together behind his back. "Evie wouldn't permit it. When we realized you had blocked everything, including the first seven years of your life, she thought it would be best for everyone if you never remembered. She instructed your teachers, all those around you, not to mention it at all. Said it had been too traumatic for you and that talking about it might send you back to the hospital, as catatonic as you had been after the murders. Of course, people talked. You know how much you've learned just from sitting in Laurie's café and listening to the old folks chatter. But most of what you've heard is probably exaggerated or just plain wrong. I couldn't convince Evie how much people would talk. She kept saying it would be old news in town within a couple of years. After a while, though, most folks forgot the real details, anyway."

"Except for you."

"David was my best friend."

"Then how could you stay away from here?"

Jake let his hands swing free and moved a little closer to her. "This ripped me apart, too, Karen. My best friend had been murdered, and I couldn't grieve in front of you or Evie. She didn't want me to come here, and…being here hurt."

Karen understood. "Which is why you took my mother's dragon box away from here."

The old man nodded. "Plus a few other things. A photo album I keep locked in the truck. Evie turned blind when it came to this place. I pushed her to sell the livestock, but I took the dog and made sure some of the important stuff, like photos, were moved to a safety-deposit box."

"Do you think she ever planned to tell me?"

"In two years, you'll take control of the estate. She'd have no choice. Although I suspect she planned to have the lawyers give you the details."

"So how does Carver Billings fit into all this?"

Jake's eyes narrowed, and Karen shrugged. She walked to the door and motioned for him to follow. "Let's find a place to sit." They left the workshop and returned to the front steps of the house, which, unlike the porch, were made of solid concrete and brick. Jake dropped down with an exhausted huff, while Karen perched, looking up at the full-leaved maple that sheltered them. "This really is a beautiful place."

"I've been told the O'Neills picked it around the turn of the century for its isolation as well as its beauty. Apparently, your great-grandfather preferred his own company."

Surprised, Karen looked around at the house. "So this place is more than one hundred years old?"

Jake picked a spot of dried clay off his shirt and flicked it away. "Yep. And it was in excellent shape before your parents died. David and Stephanie wanted to make it a showplace, but never got the chance."

Karen stood and turned, scanning the roofline, which did look solid, despite the presence of a few saplings sprouting from the gutters. "Looks like some maple seeds have gotten embedded up there."

"What did Evie tell you about the sale?"

"Not much really." Karen looked back down at Jake. "Just that Shane had sold the house to Billings. Most of what I know is what Maggie told us about them being in competition."

"David and Carver didn't care for each other. They vied for the same contracts. But I always got the impression that it was just business. Nothing personal."

"What about my father buying Aunt Evie's house? Was that personal?"

Jake remained silent a moment, then huffed again. "I should have stayed at home this afternoon." He grinned at Karen. "Are you hungry? I'm starved."

Karen grinned. "You're not trying to change the subject?"

Jake's eyes widened in mock innocence. "Me? Never. I'll talk the moon out of the sky." He pushed up from the steps. "Nope. I really am hungry. I also want to show you something. Let's go back to the retreat and get a sandwich. Need to let them know where you are, anyway, before they call out Tyler and his troops. Then we'll chat about the ins and outs of David and Evie's relationship."

ELEVEN

The color photos in the album Jake had stashed in his truck showed an extended family filled with joy. Karen recognized the grinning younger versions of Evie, Shane and her parents, who stood close, arms around each other. "That squirmy three-year-old is you." Jake pointed at a tiny blond girl who had twisted sideways in the arms of a patrician-looking woman with a bare hint of a smile. "The one afraid of showing her teeth is your grandmother Steen." The child's arms reached determinedly toward a handsome dark-haired man. Jake chuckled. "You apparently preferred your father."

Jake and Karen sat on the lodge house sofa nearest the fireplace. Maggie had left a small fire going in the grate, which Karen found oddly comforting, even though they didn't really need the heat of the flames. It made the large room feel cozier, with a warmth and comfort that the Steen home had never achieved. Maggie had also left them sandwiches, chips and tea, which remained virtually untouched as they concentrated on the album.

Karen took in all the information she could about her family and asked for more. Talking to Jake now brought back those hours in his workshop, when the topics were pottery, faith and life. "I remember her picture in one of the parlors at the house. She certainly doesn't look much like a Nana or Memaw."

Jake almost choked on his laughter. "No, Elizabeth Steen wasn't much for cutesy nicknames. She was very much the proper New England matron. You and Shane called her 'Grandmother.' She insisted on it. This was taken at a church picnic."

Karen pointed at the photo again, her finger dipping toward her father, then Evie. "They don't look like they hate each other."

Jake finally took two bites of his sandwich before answering slowly. "There is this myth around here that David and Evie didn't like each other. That wasn't quite the case."

"But I thought you said—"

Jake pushed on through her interruption. "You see, the Steens were unbelievably private. But Evie has told me things she's never told anyone, certainly not her children." He paused. "Do you know what the expression 'land rich, money poor' means?"

Karen nodded. "Old families who used to have a lot of cash but now have only land."

"That was the Steens, only no one knew. When Stephanie and David married, the Steens couldn't even pay for the wedding. That was one reason they decided to run off to California. It transferred the embarrassment away from the family, and Stephanie and David could have cared less about old proprieties."

"Is that how my father wound up buying the house?"

"More or less." Jake paused for another bite. "He and Evie got along fine at that time, although he really chafed at Mrs. Steen's meddling in his finances. Then came Mrs. Steen's diagnosis of ovarian cancer. She had no money and no insurance. Evie mortgaged the house, but eventually couldn't make the payments on both the house and the chemotherapy. At one point, they even went six months without electricity and told no one. Stephanie finally found out, and she and David got together and brought the bills up to date."

"Did the bank try to foreclose?"

"Yes. Then David got word that Carver Billings was trying to buy the mortgage. David knew Elizabeth Steen would never let *him* take care of it—"

"So SDKM did it."

Jake nodded. "With Evie's help." He abandoned the sandwich and put the plate on the end table. He settled into the couch, ready to talk at length. "David took his plan to her, and she helped him make the arrangements without her mother's knowledge. David bought the mortgage, then sold off about a hundred acres of the estate to developers. He used the money to settle the mortgage and put enough in the bank so that Evie and her mom could live mostly off the interest, as well as what meager income Mrs. Steen still got from investments her husband had made." He looked pointedly at Karen. "Your father was Evie's white knight. She had no reason to hate him. Unfortunately, it was too late. By that time, Elizabeth had stopped her treatments."

"But he never transferred the house back."

"No. Evie could do some things on her own, but she remained under her mama's thumb. David felt there was too much risk of Mrs. Steen finding out, going ballistic out of some kind of pride issues and messing up the balance again." Jake sniffed. "Controlling old woman, and yet a financial genius she wasn't."

Karen grinned. "So it wasn't only my father who didn't get along with Grandmother?"

Jake harrumphed. "That old woman could have tried the patience of the Lord Himself. She thought I was a bad influence on Evie. Probably was, though, as you can see." He smiled briefly, then continued. "After all, I never was much for money and status. Just the thought of being upstanding and proper gives me indigestion." He put a fist against his diaphragm as if he needed to burp.

"It does not!" Karen couldn't hold back her laughter.

"Does, too!" Jake's serious expression was betrayed by the shine in his eyes.

Karen sighed, the humor fading. "Was that the start of my father's competition with Carver Billings? The house?"

"More like the end." Jake stretched his right leg and massaged the knee a moment. "I'm getting too old for all this. That particular family drama took place only about six months before they died. His problems with Billings began not long after he started SDKM." He tapped the photo. "Probably around then. But the Steen estate may have been the most irritating situation. Billings wanted to buy into Mercer for years, but historic homes in this area seldom come up for public sale. They usually pass between family members, if they change hands at all."

"Why Mercer?"

"We're commuting distance from Portsmouth, Manchester and Boston. He smelled money."

"So are a lot of small towns in this area." Karen had

a hard time envisioning Mercer as a community of cluster homes and crowded subdivisions.

"But developers always seem to be looking for more."

Karen hesitated, but she had to ask. "Do you think they were killed because of business?"

He shrugged.

"But that doesn't make sense. Legitimate business-people don't just murder each other when the competition heats up!" She took a deep breath, not wanting to take the other approach any more than the rest of Mercer. "If no one had a reason to kill my father, then it had to be a random crime…or…"

Jake waited.

"Fletcher thinks it was personal, and that it was about my mother. But no one can find anyone with a reason to kill her, either."

Jake's gaze grew distant, as if he were scouring through his own set of memories from that time. "Fletcher," he said, his voice dropping, "is very good at what he does. His instincts are amazing."

"So you think he's right?"

Jake shrugged one shoulder. "I think that twenty years does not make an assumption any truer now than it did then. It could have been because of business. But it also could have been personal. We do your parents a great disservice to assume either without evidence."

Karen stood, then reached down and ran her finger over the images of her parents. "Then let's hope we can find some quickly."

"Where are you going now?"

Karen wet her lips. "Where I'd started. I need to go

back to my house, to work. I really do need to work this thing out in the clay."

"But you also need to not be alone." His concern for her was palpable. "Have someone with you, even if Jane has to camp out upstairs."

Karen hesitated, but she had to respect his love for her. "All right."

Jake watched her a moment, then nudged the photo album. "Take it with you. There are a lot of photos of your family in there. I want you to have as much time with them as you need."

Karen set her plate on the floor and closed the album, resting her hands flat on the cover. "Thank you. I'll bring it back before you know it."

Mason sat in one of Laurie's booths, his hands clutched tightly around one of her ceramic mugs, which she had kept full of coffee since he'd tripped through the door more than an hour earlier. The Federal Café, mostly empty at this time of the afternoon, echoed with the rhythmic taps of the servers' shoes and the soft clattering of the five or so diners consuming a late lunch.

He had not eaten. Could not. Maggie's sandwich now lay like a lump in his stomach. Something about the way Karen had fled, desperate to disappear into her clay work and away from the events of the day, had left his stomach sour and churning—feelings he knew were as much because of his own past as his growing emotions for the young potter.

After Jake had followed Karen, Mason had driven into town, but they weren't at the house. Desperate to trust Karen and Jake, frustrated by inactivity and frantic for information, Mason had walked the length of Mercer twice. Finally, Laurie had lassoed him, insisting he sit for a while before revisiting the house.

He stared into the cup, struggling to stay in his seat. He wanted action, to *do* something, to make sure she was still safe. The ache in his chest told him that, truly, he'd let himself go far too soon, and had not guarded his heart enough.

The steam from the coffee, the fragrant scent of the dark swirls, reminded him of his father, who had liked his coffee dark and strong, "so that a spoon would stand up in the middle," according to his mother.

He could see them in his mind, dark skin against light, the black hair of his father's Cajun ancestors blending with his mother's English blond as they held each other. They hadn't been able to be in the same room without touching each other, and their love for their son had been palpable, and so supportive it had made him feel invincible. Kisses and hugs had been frequent and open, and they'd never grown remote or distant, as Mason had seen some long-married couples do.

"I want that kind of love," he muttered into the cup. "That *exact* kind."

And the fact that he'd lost them both at the same time, precisely because they'd loved each other, remained a pain so deep in his being that he felt it every day. "Because they loved each other."

He didn't want to lose his chance at a love like that. Not like this. He had to *do* something.

Mason closed his eyes. *Lord, help me with this woman. Help me sort this out, find a way to help her. To love her as she deserves. Whatever it takes. Please.*

He opened his eyes again, the coffee still in front of him, dark and rich.

Coffee. She'd definitely go back for the Kona. Abruptly he slid out of the booth. He motioned at Laurie and left a five on the table as he strode out. He ignored her attempts to say something before he left, and his steps lengthened as he headed away from the center of town, back down the hill to Karen's cottage. He'd wait for her there.

He paused only when he saw the first wisps of smoke, the first dancing tongues of flame in her living room windows.

"No!" he screamed, then broke into a run toward the house.

The client had not lingered to see the initial burst of flame nor waited to see fire and heat demolish the little house that evoked such loathing deep within. Maybe if she hadn't made the studio so clean and airy, so perfect for pottery-making, then maybe…

Ah, such wasted thoughts. What-ifs. What if Karen hadn't become a potter? What if David and Stephanie had not died so easily? What if David had failed, even once, in his plans to take over historical New Hampshire? But, no, he had not. So unforgivable, a lack of failure in one so young.

Lack of failure creates arrogance, a sense that you can do anything you set your mind to. So it was with David O'Neill. Arrogant, so self-assured. His very attitude begged for him to be given a comeuppance.

What if I'd gone ahead and killed the seven-year-old Karen? "Should have." Then none of this would be happening. But as easy as murder had been with her parents, with Karen it had been hard. "Odd child." She'd stared, in full recognition of what she was witnessing, but with no screams, no fear, just that unblinking stare. The slap had snapped her out of it, but then Karen had just turned and fled into the yard. Catching her had put the whole thing at risk, but bending over her, whispering, "No one will believe you," had worked better than expected.

Until now.

Then one more what-if came to mind. *What if Karen was in the house?*

The client paused, then spoke aloud, reassuringly. "Of course she's not home. She's hiding. But this will kill her will. It's over. This will take care of it."

What if it does not?

The client drove on, refusing to take that line of useless thinking. No more what-ifs.

TWELVE

Karen emerged from the woods at the edge of the property in time to watch Carver Billings pull up the long, gentle curves of his driveway. She looked around at the scaffolding, where a crew of painters scrapped and repaired a facade untouched in years, and at the stunning landscape work of three gardeners so focused on their work that they did not notice the arrival of the newcomers.

Billings drove an older model Buick, and he got out, looking puzzled but curious about Karen's appearance in his yard. Karen broke into a trot, arriving at the driveway a bit breathless. "I'm sorry to trespass. I'm Karen O'Neill. There's a trail that runs adjacent—" She turned to point, but Billings interrupted her.

"Excuse me, but did you say Karen O'Neill?" The words were spoken hesitantly, but Billings's deep voice was pleasant and cultured. "David O'Neill's daughter?"

Karen looked at him uncertainly. "Uh, yes, I am. Are you Mr. Billings?"

He smiled and held out his hand. "I am. And I am very pleased to meet you, Miss O'Neill. I knew your father quite well."

Karen tucked the photo album tightly under her left arm and took Billings's hand with her right. She had no idea how to respond, then Evie's charm-school training kicked in. "My pleasure, Mr. Billings." She cleared her throat and straightened. "I had heard that you had bought this house. Welcome to Mercer."

Mr. Billings's smile widened. "Thank you. Don't mind the trespassing. The Realtor warned me about the trail, that we might see children use it on occasion."

"Shane Abernathy."

Now it was Billings's turn to look confused. "I beg your pardon?"

"Your Realtor. Shane Abernathy. Tall, thin, bald guy. Speaks as if he swallowed a thesaurus."

He chuckled at her description. "Yes, of course. I've known Shane for some time. We're in the same business. Good man. Good reputation. It's why we chose him."

"He's my cousin. I grew up with him. That's how I knew about the sale. My aunt told me."

"Mercer is quite a small town," Billings said quietly, then his smile returned and he took a deep breath. "Of course, it's why I've wanted to live here for so many years. We've visited often over the years and have many friends here. Now that my wife and I are retiring, the timing seemed perfect." He focused on Karen. "I do hope you'll come to dinner some night soon. We've almost finished redoing the dining room."

Karen paused, trying to gauge whether the invitation was genuine or just polite. Billings, his white hair a touch windblown, embodied elegance in his straight-backed stance and carefully groomed clothes. His pale blue eyes shone above the smile in a way that felt sincere to her. "I will, sir. I will call later in the week."

"Excellent! We'll make sure—" He stopped, frowning, just as Karen did, at the sound of an approaching siren. Tyler Madison's cruiser hit the Billings drive at high speed, only slowing when close to Karen and Billings. Tyler rolled down the passenger window and shouted at Karen.

"Get in!" he demanded, and she did.

"What's happened?"

Without another word, he backed out of the drive, his foot hitting the gas pedal hard.

"Tyler—"

"Let me drive." He looked over at Karen just once, then focused on the winding roads of rural Mercer.

Once was enough. Whatever had happened was bad. Karen laid the photo album on the floor, tightened her seat belt and curled against the car door, hugging herself, fighting a wave of fear that made her light-headed. One thought locked in her mind. *Please, Lord. Not Mason.*

Mason sat at the back of the ambulance, feet propped on the bumper. He held an oxygen mask to his face, but he couldn't stop staring at the flames in front of him, the monstrous red-orange claws that leaped up the side and roof of Karen's cottage, tearing it apart. The heat of the blaze had melted siding on the house next door, and the firefighters zealously fought back from the front and rear of the house. Neighbors had gathered, watching and pointing from the streets, and gasps and a few screams hit the air when the roof gave, the weight of it plowing through the blackened first floor and dropping into the basement with a roar.

Mason wanted to be numb, craved it. But he wasn't, and tears leaked from his eyes as the EMTs worked on his shoulder and left arm. Yet the tears weren't from the physical pain, sharp as that was, or the smoke that billowed around them. *I couldn't find her.* That was the pain he wanted to be numbed. *Lord, I couldn't get to her.*

He'd tried. When the fire had almost exploded in her living room, spreading quickly, his adrenaline rush had helped him break in the door, causing a backflash that had singed his hair and sent him reeling backward. Still, he'd pushed forward, entering the house, screaming her name. She *had* to be there. Where else would she be?

The fire had already blocked the stairs to the second floor, and he couldn't get past it. The floor beneath his feet had begun to crack and give when he'd headed downstairs, where he'd found himself trapped. The fire had seemed almost alive as it had lapped through the ceiling and crawled down the wallboards of the studio. Something liquid and melting had poured down the staircase behind him. He'd broken out one of the windows to escape, collapsing in the backyard, coughing and gagging from smoke inhalation. He didn't remember getting hurt, but his left shoulder throbbed, and there were cuts and scrapes up and down his left side and arm.

Please, not upstairs. Don't let her be upstairs. His fervent prayers felt like the pleas of a child. *Save her.*

"*Save them,*" the teenaged Mason had begged the firefighters who'd rushed to his own home. His father, ordering his son to stay and wait for the emergency teams, had gone back in the blazing house to get his wife. Neither had returned. Later, Mason had spent days sifting through the ashes, looking for any sign of his past, anything that looked familiar. Nothing had remained. Only their wedding rings, which the coroner had given to Mason after the funerals.

"Please, not again." Mason's voice, muffled by the mask, sounded distant and hollow.

The EMT looked at him, her eyes filled with concern. "We need to get you to the hospital."

Mason shook his head. "I can't leave. Not yet."

"Mason!" The scream, high-pitched, feminine and desperate, jerked Mason to his feet. He turned toward the sound to see Karen racing toward him, hair flying, feet stumbling over hoses and equipment. He dropped the mask and ran, his chest tight with relief. He caught her up in his arms, his tears wetting her hair and face as he held her as tightly as he could.

"You're safe! Thank God you're safe!" He kissed her hair, her cheeks, showering her with the grateful relief that seared through him. "*Chère, ma chère,* I thought you were in the house!"

"You went in!" she yelled at him. "Tyler said you went in after me!" Tears streamed down her cheeks, and she suddenly pushed back at him, smacking his chest. "You idiot! I could have lost you, too!"

She hit him again, and he caught her hands and held them against his chest with one hand, stroking her face with the other. "I had to."

"But the house was on fire!" At that moment her own words seemed to sink in, and her eyes widened as she turned, looking past him. "My house!" She screamed again, and lurched toward the flames.

Two firefighters, hearing her scream, turned to block her, but Mason held tight, pulling her against his chest, holding her arms down. "It's gone," he whispered. "I'm sorry. I tried."

Karen's sobs rocked her now, and her knees gave way. Mason eased both of them to the ground, still cradling her against him. She clung to him, fingers curled like claws into his shirt and skin. He didn't even feel the pain. All that mattered was her. *"Chère,"* he whispered over and over as he stroked her hair and back, trying to give her comfort.

A few moments later Tyler approached and draped a thick woolen blanket around both of them. Mason looked up with wordless thanks, and Tyler nodded, his face somber. He left them and went to stand next to a man in a firefighter's uniform. He directed the action, his only equipment a handheld radio. He and Tyler spoke in low tones, and the fireman handed Tyler a small slip of paper, then pointed toward one corner of the house.

That's where it had begun, Mason thought, remembering how the flames had birthed in that corner and spread across the living room. Arson.

Mason tightened his hold on the sobbing Karen and kissed the top of her head again, his sense of relief still more powerful than any physical pain, anger at the attack or sympathy for her loss. She was still there, and in that moment, that was what mattered most.

He watched the dying flames as her sobbing slowly ceased. They subsided almost at the same time, the red and yellow flickers slowly consumed by black smoke as Karen's grief evolved from racking sobs to silent shivers of grief. Finally, with a long, shuddering sigh, she raised her head and looked, first at him, then around her.

When she spoke, her whispered words cracked and

broke in the heated air. "How do I tell him that I'll stop? How do I make him leave us alone?"

"I don't know. But we'll find a way."

She leaned her head against his chest, and her grip eased, becoming less desperate. "What do I do now?"

Mason knew the feeling all too well. The loss, the feeling of being adrift, with no home or focus. Or hope. "I don't know. But whatever you need to do, I'll help," he whispered into her hair. "I promise you."

Standing at the edge of the crowd, Luke Knowles's client tried to avoid grinning, but the sense of success, of winning, was almost overwhelming. Seeing Karen slumped against that stupid boy—he had run into the burning house! Fool!—the client knew the final goal had been achieved.

Message received! She would stop making those wicked vases and move on with her life. With luck, she'd even leave Mercer, maybe move into Boston or New York with the writer, and they'd both starve in some little hovel of an apartment. Sweet revenge for all that had come before.

All right, no, that fantasy would never come to be, not with the inheritance lurking two years out. Still. Life *would* return to normal.

Strange thought, that. Normal. Hmph. *Normal* had nearly always been a burden, a requirement when the client had wanted nothing more than adventure, travel, new romance, excitement, a life of thrills in some far-off exotic port. Now, after all this, *normal* had become a craving worthy of a man in a desert thirsting for a few drops of water.

Amused by the idea, the client moved through the crowd slowly. Must offer condolences. After all, it would be bad manners to be there and not reach out to someone so close, so beloved by the community, who was undergoing such trauma. It would be an easily noticed oversight.

As the bright light of the fire diminished, the crowd began to part, and the client soon reached the grieving couple, both of whom were being helped into an ambulance. As the EMTs finished their work, the client reached out and touched Karen's leg.

"Karen, I'm sorry. Please let me know if there's anything I can do…."

THIRTEEN

Mason stood at the edge of the yard, looking over the devastated ruins of Karen's cherished home. The charred beams and thick piles of ashes still smoldered, a dark smoke eking out of the blackness and up toward the deep purple of the dawn sky. His mind reeled to remember that only two days ago he'd stood there, preparing himself to tell her about Luke Knowles. Unbelievable how much had changed.

The night before felt like a twisted, smothering dream. Doctors had treated both of them in the emergency room—Karen for her hysteria and him for burns, cuts and smoke inhalation. He felt not one moment of regret, despite the continual sting of the injuries and the lingering heaviness in his lungs. He knew now three things that he'd doubted before: his feelings for Karen ran deeper than he'd been able to accept; he could, in fact, be as devoted to someone as his father had been; and he could finally understand the faith of his mother, of Karen, in a God who loved him.

But what did that mean going forward?

Karen appeared to accept that they both cared more for each other than they had wanted to admit after such a short friendship. At the hospital, she'd been unable to leave his side, so loudly determined to stay with him that they had treated them both in the same room.

They were now bonded by something stronger than friendship, solidified by trial. "As clay is stronger from the fire." Her description, muttered last night, just before the sedation they had given her had taken effect. Now she lay in her bed at the retreat, drugged into the rest she would not have otherwise gotten.

Mason, however, couldn't rest and refused to take the pain pills the doctor had offered. He wanted every sense aware and alert this morning. He had work to do.

The sun still had not risen above the trees in Karen's backyard, and a chill mist hung in the air. Under other circumstances, the early morning would have felt refreshing. Now the lack of sleep made Mason's eyes itch almost as much as the remaining drifts of smoke.

Later that morning, he knew the fire chief and Tyler would be back to examine the ruins for signs of arson, and the area would be off-limits until they finished. His work, however, needed to be done before Karen emerged from her drugged sleepiness, before she settled too securely into the decision she'd made last night in the depths of the fire-driven trauma.

She'd resolved to quit pottery. Not just the face vases, but all of it. In her despair and confusion over all the events swirling around her, she'd become convinced that this wasn't just about her parents or her face vases. Someone hated *her*. So by the time they had arrived at the ER, her decision to stop making the face vases had expanded to include all pottery. To Karen, the fire represented something more than a single individual driven to stop her from creating one type of vase. She saw it instead as guidance from God that she should abandon the artistic life entirely.

The anger that now coursed through Mason felt as scorching as the blaze that had consumed her home. Mason's belief in God now ran deeper than ever before. And he knew to the core of his soul that this had less to do with God's guidance than the wickedness of one person.

Now if he could just prove it.

As if on a mission, Mason strode down the slant of the front lawn, skirting the ruins and trying not to slip on ground turned into a mush of mud and blackened grass by the fire and the firefighters. The granite hillside into which the house had been built had been stripped in several places down to the rock by the trucks and falling beams. The back wall, being mostly glass, had collapsed first, causing the roof to angle down and slide across the outside walls into the backyard, where it had continued to burn separately until extinguished by the fire team. Walking to the back, and picking his way between the remains of the roof and the basement floor, he found he had a better view of the destruction.

The house was a total loss. Parts of the front and north walls still stood, but the rest had plunged into the basement, including major portions of both floors. To his right, he could see the remnants of one kiln, its firebricks charred but unbroken, protected by a floor joist that had dropped at an angle, still supported on the front by the immovable granite that had served as the front wall of the studio. And therein lay Mason's greatest hope.

The granite baffle.

Even now, with the violet of dawn giving way to a

pale gold, the narrow entrance to Karen's secret storage room was barely visible. Mason took a circuitous route to it, avoiding other angled and creaking joints and sections of wall and floor. The sturdiness of the solid rock beneath his feet had a reassuring effect on him, but he still took no chances with fire-ravaged remains around him.

Reaching the entrance, he touched the wall gingerly, half expecting it to still be hot. Yet it was already cool, and Mason turned sideways, edging his way inside. Because it had been cut completely out of the rock, the storage room had a ceiling of solid granite, and the baffle turn meant little light came from outside. Knowing the room would be almost pitch-black, Mason had brought a flashlight, which he now pulled from his pocket and snapped on. A scent of smoke hung in the air, but the bright, thin beam of his light revealed exactly what he'd hoped.

All of Karen's storage boxes were still intact. The same baffle that kept out light had kept out fire and most of the water. Some of the boxes closest to the door had bowed and warped from the heat, but the ones at the very back of the room, a full eight feet from the Z-shaped baffle, showed no signs that they'd been through a fire at all. He flipped the latch on one and opened it, eagerly rummaging through the contents. Through his fingers slid picture after picture of vases, platters and bowls.

A cough of laughter pushed through Mason's anger, and an unexpected joy came over him as he clutched a handful of photos. "Thank You, Lord!" he exclaimed.

Holding the flashlight in his teeth, Mason gathered

several boxes in his arms, beginning the long task of emptying the room and carrying the contents to his car at the top of the hill.

Karen struggled out of her medicine-induced sleep, groaning as she rolled over in bed, stiff from lying too long in one position. Parched by the aftereffects both of the medicine and of crying half the night, her mouth felt as if every surface had become swollen and sore. The dryness in her throat made her want to cough—an action that made a vise of pain circle her skull. Karen buried her face in the pillow, and tears once again soaked the pillowcase. Being awake hurt.

Even more excruciating, however, was the cruelty of the previous night's events, a reality that seeped slowly through her exhaustion. Her home had been destroyed by fire, taking with it everything she owned. Everything she was.

Being a potter wasn't just what she did for a living—it was the center of her being. The art that emerged from the clay, coaxed by her fingers and palms, also came from within her mind and heart. They were the reflections of ideas she had, colors she loved, shapes that entranced her. From the time Jake had shown her what to do, how she could focus with the clay in a way she'd not been able to before, Karen knew she had been born to be a potter. It went deeper than just knowledge; she believed with all her heart that this was God's design for her, His chosen path for her life.

Giving it up meant walking away from all her dreams, all her beliefs for her life. Yet how could she continue when it had meant the destruction of everything—and possibly everyone—she loved? Clearly, whoever hated her and her work would not stop until she did.

The whirling speculations in Karen's mind came to an abrupt halt as another thought occurred to her, a question no one had yet asked. The curiosity of it pushed her further awake, and she sat up, trying to ignore the spinning room and the ache in her skull. As she sat on the edge of her bed, trying to orient herself, a soft tap on the door was followed by Maggie opening it quietly and peering in. When she saw Karen, she stepped fully inside, carrying a tray of tea and crackers.

"I'm glad you're awake. Can you eat something?"

"Yes," Karen whispered, not trusting herself to nod.

"Tea and aspirin for your head. Saltines for your tummy." She sat the tray on the night table and poured tea from a steaming pot into a delicate china cup. She added sugar and a dollop of milk, then passed it to Karen.

Karen sipped. "How did you know what would help?"

"Experience." Just the one word, and both of them dropped the subject. Karen had heard enough about the events surrounding Aaron Jackson's death to know that Maggie had been through some rough times herself. She held out her hand as Maggie shook two aspirin from a small bottle. The crackers lay in a fan on a saucer, and Maggie held it as Karen took the aspirin, then picked up a cracker to nibble on.

Maggie waited silently until about half the cracker had disappeared. "Do you think you're up to coming out to the living room? We really need to talk to you."

Karen hesitated. "It's over. You know that. I'm done with it all."

Maggie watched her eat the rest of the cracker and drink a few more sips of tea. "We'd still like to talk."

Karen took a long, deep breath, a little surprised that her head didn't protest. "Okay. I also have a question to ask everyone."

"Good. Do you want help getting dressed?"

The tea felt so warm and comforting, Karen didn't want to move at all. Still… "Yes, please."

Mason paced from the glass wall at the front of the lodge to the one at the back, then turned and started over. Fletcher stood looking out one of the rear windows, so motionless that Mason wondered if he were still awake, especially after having driven from Boston earlier that morning. Tyler sat at the dining table, flipping through a photo album that he said Karen had left in his car. He paused more than once, scowling at a page, then turned to the next photo.

Mason paused, looking first down the hallway toward Karen's room, then at Fletcher and Tyler. "Do you think we should—"

"No." Fletcher turned from the window, his voice flat. "Let Maggie work her medicine. She's very good at this, very soothing for people who are hurting." He paused, glancing at the stack of metal boxes on the table. "You are just a touch agitated this morning."

Tyler caught the implication and looked up from the album. "Agitated." He scowled again at Mason. "You should *not* have gone back in that house. If that messes with the fire chief's investigation, he'll have both our heads on a platter."

Mason crossed his arms. "You didn't see her last

night. And I didn't touch anything to do with the fire. Just the boxes. I had to do something. I've never seen a woman so devastated."

Tyler and Fletcher exchanged a quick glance but said nothing.

"Look who I found," Maggie said gently.

They all turned, and Mason felt his heart ache. A slow-moving Karen entered from the hallway, a true picture of dejection with her shoulders slumped and her face the color of bleached cloth. "Sorry, I'm moving a little slow," she said, her voice a bare whisper. "My head's still a little unsure from the med—" Her words broke off and her mouth went slack as her gaze swung to the neat stacks of boxes on the table. She reached a hand toward them. "How—?" Then she stared at Mason, her gaze taking him in from head to toe. "You did this."

He suddenly felt conspicuous in his soot-covered jeans and shirt. "I had to." He crossed to her and took her hands. "Please listen to me." He pulled her, steadily but gently, toward the table. "I've said this to you before, and I know Jake has said it hundreds of times, but now I really want you to listen. I want you to *hear*.

"God gave you something incredibly special. Even you yourself said that there are people who can make pots, but the clay doesn't sing for them. It's just a craft that they can do well. But you have a gift, something that comes from the depths of your spirit. Your art speaks to me. Why do you think I kept pursuing it, wanting more people to discover it? You don't think I meet hundreds of artists in what I do? A lot of people try, but only a few can do what you do—as you said, out of your imagination and a bit of raw clay. It speaks to the depths of those who love your work, who buy it not just because it's pretty but because it strikes at something in their souls."

They reached the table, and he pulled out a chair and guided her to sit. Then he pulled the closest box to the edge of the table and opened it. He forced her to take a handful of photos, then spread others from the box in a fan shape across the table. "Look at what you've achieved. Look at what you've done that no one else can do because God gave no one else your soul, your heart, your mind."

He pointed to the boxes. "There are seventeen boxes, hundred of photos. That's hundreds of pots and vases and platters and plaques and urns. All from you. Because God made you, Karen O'Neill, and no one else can do what you do. Just you. Please don't quit being who God made you to be."

Karen looked at the photos, her fingers closing tightly around the ones in her hands. Then she raised her head, her eyes bright with tears. "I don't want you to get hurt."

Mason knelt in front of her, his hands grasping her wrists. "I'm not going to get hurt. We will catch whoever is doing this. Don't let this make you stop."

Karen gazed at him a moment, then looked up and around, pausing in turn at Maggie, Tyler and Fletcher. She stayed with Fletcher a moment, then she spoke, her voice gaining strength. "Something occurred to me this morning." She cleared her throat. "How does this person know I haven't already quit? What made him burn my house? How did he know that he hadn't already succeeded in making me stop?"

Fletcher and Tyler exchanged glances again, then

Fletcher moved closer, pulling a chair from under the table and sitting at Karen's side, opposite Mason. He leaned forward, bracing his elbows on his knees. "Because he's been watching every move you make. He, if it is a he, has seen that you are still trying to beat this."

Tyler stepped closer, as well. "While you were sleeping, and *you* were robbing crime scenes—" he threw a harsh look at Mason "—my guys have been busy. They found a cluster of footprints on the trail near your house, as if someone had stood there for a long time. They found the same footprints all along the trail, from your house to here…" He paused and crossed his arms. "And another cluster at the farmhouse."

Karen turned to him. "The farmhouse? Are you sure? When?"

Tyler shrugged. "We can't tell when, but the cluster at the farmhouse was the kicker, the proof we needed that the prints on the trail were related to what's happened with you. There'd be no reason for a casual hiker to be hanging out, watching that farmhouse."

"They're also a distinctive print," Fletcher explained. "Peg insists that it's one of the more expensive Merrell hiking boots, but none of us know Merrell from a flip-flop. We faxed the prints to New York, in case they can track purchases to anyone with a New Hampshire address."

Mason stood. "But whoever this is knows the area well. Knows that trail."

Tyler nodded. "And I'd say they know the entire family."

"Did you find anything on David's computer?" Mason asked Fletcher.

The detective straightened. "Ah, yes, the computer.

My friend did, in fact, retrieve most of David's files. He's going to convert them to modern programs and return them to you for your records. No major breakthroughs. David kept a fine set of books, everything clean and aboveboard. No great secrets, death threats or sneaky dealings." He turned to Karen, one corner of his mouth upturned. "He was writing a children's book with you as the heroine. Nothing turned up on the cash, either."

"Nothing about Carver Billings?" Karen asked.

Fletcher shook his head. "Only the usual correspondence between competitive businessmen. We did find a list of the open houses David had planned for that month, including the address for the one he hosted the day he died."

Tyler put his hand on her shoulder. "Which leads us to the hardest question. Would you be willing to go back to that house?"

Karen's eyes widened, and Mason could see the fear growing in her face, feel the tension in her arms. "Why?"

"Do you remember," Fletcher said softly, "what happened at the farmhouse? How the memories came flooding back?"

Karen stood, pulling away from Mason and letting the photos drift to the floor. "You can't ask me to remember that. You can't!"

Fletcher stood with her. "I think your subconscious has been going there for a while, Karen. It may be time—"

"No!"

Maggie stepped between the men and Karen. "Time out, guys." She put a calming hand on Karen's arm. "I know you want to catch whoever's doing this. But one trauma at a time, shall we?"

"Let me take you to Jake's." Mason reached out, as if to take Karen's hand.

They all stood silent for a moment, but Mason could see the edgy fear begin to drain away from Karen, and he stepped closer. "Not to the house. To the studio."

Still, she remained wary. "Why?"

His voice dropped in volume and tone. He so wanted to comfort her! "Because I think you need the clay." He paused, then pushed the thought again. "You need the clay."

They waited, and Mason watched a half-dozen emotions play across Karen's face. Doubt. Fear. Desire. When he saw the desire, the need, he knew for certain that he'd been right.

"Let me get some shoes." Karen turned and left the room.

Fletcher and Tyler immediately turned on Mason. "Be careful," Fletcher warned him. "The killer may think she's defeated after last night, but that doesn't mean she's not still being watched." He focused again on Tyler. "I'll contact the owners of the house where her parents died. She may come around sooner rather than later."

Tyler agreed. "I'm going to check with the fire chief." He returned to the table, his hand resting thoughtfully on the photo album Jake had given Karen. "I'm going to take this, as well, if no one objects. And some of the photos from the house." No one answered, as no one objected. Maggie brought him a bag from the kitchen about the same time that Karen emerged again from her bedroom. This time her shoulders were set, her mouth in a firm line. "Let's go."

* * *

The client sighed as Laurie set a breakfast plate on the table. Success made life so much brighter, more fun to indulge in the little pleasures—like French toast at the Federal Café.

Remaining close to Karen O'Neill had been a serious risk, especially with all those vases floating about. But she apparently had not made the connection between the face on the vase and the face in her past until quite recently.

A snarl curled the corner of the client's mouth. Mason DuBroc recent, as a matter of fact. What a mistake that was! He certainly looked and sounded like a dolt from Hicksville. Who knew he'd be the one to draw the lines between the dots and connect vases with faces with events. And so quickly that plans had to be escalated, if only to ensure the success of defeating Karen's dreams to become the next big thing in the art world.

Insurance. *Hmm.* There was a pause in the eating. That article about those blasted vases had been well written with an intriguing amount of detail and historical references. DuBroc seemed to be an expert at research and well skilled at linking cause and effect. Unlike Karen O'Neill, whose notorious lack of focus had even made it into DuBroc's article; the good professor had a bit of a ferret in him, a determination to get to the mole, no matter how deep the hole.

The client almost laughed at the image. Still, if the boy truly had fallen in love with the artist, he could remain a problem long after the pottery had ceased to be.

The cup of coffee paused in midair. Perhaps a little more insurance was called for after all.

FOURTEEN

Mason's words echoed in Karen's mind as they drove to the Steen estate. They had struck hard, sounding so much like Jake's advice earlier in her career that they had made the hairs on her neck stand up. They began the drive in silence, pulling away from the retreat in Mason's sports car, both facing stonily ahead. As the woodland gave way to the small-town streets, however, Karen looked over at him.

Soot still stained his clothes in random patches, and smears blotched his forehead and cheeks. The morning mist had dampened his thick hair, and the small curls at the ends of his hair caressed his neck and jawline. One dropped repeatedly over his right eye, ignoring his efforts to keep it pushed out of the way.

She pursed her lips, wanting to say something, yet almost everything in her head felt weak in the wake of his earlier speech and the determination of all three men to see this through to the end. Finally, what came out was a murmur barely louder than the car's humming engine. "Thank you."

He looked at her, his dark eyes intense. He pushed the curl back and opened his mouth to speak, then closed it again. He turned quickly to look back at the road, causing the curl to drop again.

"I would do anything for you."

She reached up and brushed the curl back. "I know."

With an action both forceful and affectionate, Mason clasped her hand in his, pressing it to his lips. Every muscle in Karen's body tensed at the soft, brief touch, and she realized that she, too, would do anything for this man at her side.

"Lord," she whispered. "Please get us through this in one piece."

Mason lowered their hands to the console between the seats but did not release hers. His eyes sparkled as he glanced at her again. "Amen."

He finally let go as they reached the Steen driveway. He turned into it, driving this time all the way to the back, parking next to Jake's studio. They got out and entered without knocking.

Jake stood at the sink, cleaning a few of his tools, the running water masking the sound of their entry. Yet when he turned and saw them, he showed no surprise. "I've been expecting you," he said, his rough baritone both serious and welcoming. "Evie told me about the fire. She and Shane were both there."

Karen nodded, remembering the pale faces among the crowd. "I know. I saw them. Along with half the town. Even the newcomers."

"I'm sorry."

"I need the clay."

Jake dried his hands on a ratty towel and motioned toward his worktable. "I've already cut three sections off. All brown, but I have red and white if you need them."

Karen picked up one of the dark chunks of raw clay and hefted it, bouncing it in one hand a moment, then switching hands. She dropped it back on the table with a dull thud, then stripped off her outer shirt and pulled her T-shirt from the waist of her jeans, fluffing it a bit.

"I'll get you a bat and some water. Center wheel?"

"Yes, thanks," she replied, though she barely noticed his movements as he placed a round bat in the middle of his three wheels. Her focus was now solely on the clay, her clay. She rolled it on the table, kneading it until the texture felt right, a soft firmness that she liked and could sense under her fingers, yet could never describe to anyone else. Karen dropped the ball onto the center of the bat with a solid thump. Her foot found the wheel's pedal almost out of instinct, and she centered the clay, then wet her hands and cupped both around the ball, increasing the speed of the wheel. The earth under her hands seemed to come alive, shifting and changing with the least touch. "What are you?" she whispered. "What do you need to be?"

Tall. She coaxed it, the clay building upon itself. Holding both hands around it to steady its growth, a pillar emerged, elegant and stable. She paused, watching it spin. "What kind?" In her mind she saw it, a vase, but not one of her face vases. They were broad and sturdy, with the thicker walls needed to support the faces, which were hand-built and added later. This one was slender and elegant, like her aunt Evie. The face vases were also wild and kaleidoscopic with their colors, bright reds and greens. This one would have red streaks, but the base would be emerald green, that special glaze that Jake kept, which went on black but fired the color of Shane's favorite sweater or Carver Billings's Buick, or the pants…

The pants.

A vision flashed in front of her face. Legs walking toward her face. Emerald green. Sweatpants. Blood splatters. Green and red streaks…no, green *with* red streaks…

Karen heard herself scream, but she only saw her hands crushing the clay, the wheel grinding to a halt, her fingers buried deep in the earth. Tears blurred her vision and she fought to stay upright but couldn't. She weaved, and strong arms wrapped around her, pulling her down to a sitting position on the ground. The clay came with her, the ball landing heavily in her lap.

"Chère." She looked up to see Mason's face close, his expression so fraught with anxiety that she wanted to touch him, but her hands remained weighted by the clay. Her breath was so rapid she felt as if she were panting.

"The house!" Her words sounded like a wheeze, but she had to get them out. "I have to go to that house!"

Mason pulled Karen to her feet with Jake's help, both of them watching her for signs of dizziness or instability on her feet. Her scream had turned every one of his nerves inside out. Whatever she'd seen had shaken her to the core. They escorted her to the sink, where Jake scraped the clay from her hands and held them under the water until the last morsel of earth had washed away.

"What house?" Jake asked, as Karen dried her hands and Mason found her a stool to perch on.

"The house." Karen inhaled deeply, shakily.

Obviously, she still felt rattled. Mason hovered just behind her left shoulder, until she reached out and took his hand. "I'm okay," she said, looking up at him. "I just saw something… The clay brought it out…"

Jake nodded. "It has a way of doing that. What did you see?"

"Legs. It must have been after the murder, when I was out in the yard."

The older man's eyebrows went up. "Just legs?"

"Not exactly. Pants, actually. Emerald-green sweat-pants. You know, the fleece kind, but without the elastic around the ankles. They had blood on them." She looked up at Mason again. "I think Fletcher's right. I think I'm close to remembering. The house might help."

Karen gripped Mason's arm. "Do you have your cell phone?" He nodded and she continued. "Call Fletcher and get the address, will you?" She turned back to Jake as Mason pulled out his phone. She pulled Jake into a tight hug. "Thank you, for everything."

Mason dialed slowly, watching as Jake returned Karen's hug with fatherly affection. "Be careful, girl. You've been holding in a poison for a long time. Be careful that it's not you that gets stung."

Karen looked at him, a little puzzled by the remark. "I will."

A dark voice buzzed in Mason's ear. "Fletcher Mac-Allister." Mason turned away, and didn't hear if Karen and Jake said anything else.

Fifteen minutes later, they were at the retreat, trans-ferring to Fletcher's larger, distinctly nondescript car. Fletcher teased Mason as he locked up the sports car. "Did you just have to buy arrest-me red when you got that thing? Not very practical."

Mason snorted. "Of course. I'm not very practical, remember? I majored in art history."

"Where's the house, Fletcher?" Karen settled in the front passenger's seat and fastened her belt.

The tall detective folded himself into the car and did the same. "Ridgeview Estates. Back in the mid-eighties, it was a new development." He glanced in the rearview mirror to make sure Mason was also buckled in before starting the car. "The open house was in a spec home at the back of the development."

"*Spec* meaning…?" Karen prompted.

"Built to sell from ready. Most developments, you go in and buy a plot of land and a house plan based on the models you view. Then the contractor builds your home the way you want it. Spec homes are built without buyers signed up. Most developers build one or two."

Fletcher pulled out of the retreat and turned away from Mercer. "This home was toward the back of the development, and had only one neighbor at the time. According to your father's notes, he was the broker of record for the development. Semi-steady sales, and it gave him time to work on ideas for SDKM. He had disagreed with the developer over having a spec home so far back in the complex, and he suspected it might have been for a relative who backed out of the deal. I found evidence that your dad was doing everything he could to sell the home but without a lot of luck." Fletcher made a right turn and headed up a slight incline.

"I suppose they checked out the developer after the murders," Mason said.

Fletcher nodded. "As best they could. He never was much of a suspect. He and his wife were in Florida at the time, checking out retirement homes." He glanced at Karen. "Part of the reason the cops had problems solving this is that they couldn't find anyone who hated your parents. Except for Carver Billings, David kept his business as low-key as possible, probably to keep Elizabeth Steen from getting curious."

Karen sat a bit straighter in her seat. "Okay, I'm going to ask because no one else seems to want to." She faced Fletcher. "We've gone around and around the pros and cons of who could have done this. Aunt Evie had motive, but there's no evidence. Daddy's business could have been the cause, but there's no evidence. Now. What's the likelihood that Carver Billings actually did kill my parents?"

Fletcher's mouth tightened, and Mason watched him in the rearview mirror, admiring the man's self-control. "As you pointed out, the problem," Fletcher said evenly, "is with the evidence. Circumstantially, he would definitely be a 'person of interest.' But there's nothing physical, nothing forensic to connect him."

Karen let out a frustrated sigh. "Or *any*body! So no matter what I remember, the killer could still go free."

"Unless what you remember points to some kind of evidence." At the top of the incline, a faded and cracked subdivision sign announced that they had arrived at Ridgeview Estates, Modern Homes For The Twentieth-Century Family. For Sale By Owner signs clustered around the foot of the larger sign, their arrows all pointing into the subdivision. Fletcher turned, then slowed, checking a small slip of paper lying on the front seat. "It's 1412 Essex. Ridgeview Boulevard to Wilmot to Essex."

Fortunately, Wilmot went only to the left, and the right onto Essex took them to a cul-de-sac at the rear of the subdivision. The houses, midsize ranch homes fronted by vinyl siding and dubious landscaping, showed their age with mold on the gutters and cracks in the sidewalks and driveways. Most of the lawns were neatly cut and edged, but the homes seemed to belong to folks with more stuff than the houses could hold. Toys and lawn equipment spilled out of garages and onto the drives and yards.

The house at 1412 Essex had been cared for more expertly than most on the street. "Retired couple," Fletcher explained, as they parked and got out. "They plan to stay here until they have to move into assisted living, and they have more time to take care of the house. They're the only owners the house has had. Bought it not long after the crime scene cleanup crew had finished." He parked the car near the mailbox. "When I called, they weren't surprised. They knew the history of the house and told me they'd been expecting such a call for years. They left a key under a chair cushion on the sun porch."

He led the way around the back of the house, where they found the door to a pleasantly furnished, glassed-in sun porch unlocked. The warm and comfortable room did come complete with a key under the pink flowered cushion of an equally pink wicker chair. Fletcher stopped and pointed toward the backyard, a broad strip of grass that ended at dense woods running the length of the property.

"These houses are a bit more prized because most of that area is common grounds for the complex. So you wind up with a lot of lawn that you don't have to take care of and a great view." He pointed toward a slight rise in the ground. "They found you there, Karen, about fifty feet from the house, close to the woods. They think the culprit walked right by you. They found blood drops leading from the house into the trees."

Mason watched as Karen stepped toward the glass, her hand reaching out. Color drained from her face, and the fingers that seemed to be trying to reach back through time trembled. He put his hand on her back. "Are you sure you're up to this?"

She continued to gaze into the past. "Do you remember this morning, when you said you had to go after those boxes? You *had* to?"

"Yes."

She faced him, her eyes dark blue and moist. "I have to, Mason. What I saw this morning with the clay… I know I can never go back to the pottery unless I do this. And I know now that this is the time. While you are here with me. I *have* to."

She turned and followed Fletcher into the house. Mason hesitated, glancing back to the yard. *While you are here with me.* The confidence in the words made him want to take every step right alongside her.

"Hide her and keep her," he muttered, and entered the house.

The back door led to a small dining area, separated from the galley-style kitchen by a bar. Directly in front of them, on the other side of the kitchen, was a tidy living room.

A hallway led from the living room down to two other bedrooms and a bath, and Mason heard Karen checking out each room. He and Fletcher watched as she eased through the house, her actions more like those of a terrified seven-year-old girl than a twenty-eight-year-old woman. She peered around every corner, as if expecting someone to charge out and grab her. Mason's chest tightened as the pictures from Evie's photo album dashed through his mind. Karen as a child, a blond doll with a bright smile and far too much sadness in her eyes.

"Cui bono?" Fletcher asked. When Mason looked at him, puzzled by the Latin phrase, Fletcher shrugged one shoulder. "First question any lawyer asks. Who would benefit most from their deaths? Evie? Billings? Someone else we've not thought about?"

Karen's head appeared around the frame of the door separating the kitchen from the den. "As many times as we've asked, I don't know, really." She paused, that long-ago sadness returning to her eyes. "Maybe there is more about my parents we don't know." She looked around. "I had to come, but maybe it's too soon. We don't know enough."

Fletcher shook his head. "Unless your father had personal conflicts we've not been able to uncover, I've always thought it was personal, ever since I read the cold-case file, and saw the descriptions of the wounds…" He paused. "Are you sure you want to do this?"

Karen stepped back into the kitchen, her face solemn. "I did it almost every night for years after, Fletcher. No matter how hard I tried, I couldn't remember. When the nightmares started, I tried even harder. Nothing. Then I found that pottery helped the nightmares. Since then, remembering didn't seem important." She paused and took a deep breath. "Now it does."

He looked her over carefully, then nodded. He squared his shoulders and led them back into the living room. "They think your mother was stabbed first." He turned slightly and swung his arms over an area in the middle of the room. "About here. Best guess is that she was facing that way." He pointed at the back door.

"The front door would have been standing open," Mason said softly. "Since it was an open house."

Fletcher nodded. "And she either didn't hear the killer come in, or…"

"Or she knew them well enough to turn her back on them," Karen finished.

"Yes." Fletcher hesitated, looking Karen over again closely.

"I'm okay," she reassured him.

He wet his lips and continued. "There were slight wounds on the back of her shoulders and neck—faint cuts that look almost as if the attacker didn't really know the strength it takes to kill someone, or didn't really want to kill her…at first. The fatal wounds were on the front, as if your mother had been attacked from behind, then turned to defend herself." He turned toward the front door. "She had defensive wounds on her hands and arms."

They followed as Fletcher walked back through the kitchen and into a small den. He pointed to a door on the far wall. "Your father may have been in the master bedroom suite and heard your mother's screams. He was killed here in the den." Fletcher paused again, his eyes watching Karen steadily. "But your father was only stabbed twice in the chest."

Karen chewed her lower lip. Mason stepped toward her protectively, but she shook her head and he stopped. "So my mother was attacked like that because an inexperienced killer got to her first?"

Fletcher looked down at the ground, as if deciding

how much to say. "The attack on your dad was clean. Almost sterile. Two wounds that went directly between the ribs into the heart." He crossed to her, his voice low and gentle, despite his words. "This wasn't an inexperienced killer, but the murders were substantially different. Your father's was clean and quick, just two wounds, one probably for insurance. The killer just wanted him dead and out of the way. Your mother's death had passion in it."

"What about two killers?" Mason asked. "It would explain why David didn't make it any farther than the den once the attack on his wife started."

Fletcher nodded. "It would. And it would make sense if this were, in fact, a random crime of opportunity. But why kill with such passion if you just want money? Why not just rob them?"

Karen's eyes scanned the walls, and Mason couldn't tell if she was remembering the house as it had been or if she just didn't want to look at Fletcher. Her voice had taken on a tear-choked hoarseness. "You're saying that whoever did this wanted my father dead but my mother punished. This was about her." She swallowed. "Aunt Evie and Billings benefit if this is business, but who would want to kill my mother? Who could possibly benefit? She was a stay-at-home mom. She took me to dance class and acting lessons. We would go to the park. I never heard her have a fight with anyone, not even my dad. In fact, the only time I remember her even raising her voice was when…"

Karen's voice faded to a harsh whisper and her eyes went distant. "The vases…the faces…those white streaks…" She stopped and her eyes widened as a look of horrible recognition clouded her face. "Oh, no!" she whispered.

Fletcher took a step toward her, questions obviously on the tip of his tongue.

The step saved Karen's life.

Behind him, the window at the back of the den popped, and Fletcher cried out as a bullet sheared through his shoulder before embedding itself in the kitchen door frame, only inches from Karen's head. Karen's screams filled Mason's ears as he grabbed her, throwing both of them to the floor. Fletcher fell heavily beside them.

The windowpane, which had split top to bottom from the first hit, fell out of the frame as another bullet buried itself in the far wall. A fiery sting seared Mason's scalp, and blood flowed down one side of his head. As the first red drops hit Karen's cheek, she reached for his face, her hand pressing hard against his wound.

"Get into the kitchen!" Fletcher rolled onto one side, breathing heavily, grasping his shoulder. "Behind the bar."

Mason and Karen scrambled on hands and knees back into the narrow room, and a torrent of Cajun-accented French ripped from Mason, most of which had little to do with protecting Karen and everything to do with taking care of whoever wanted her dead. Fletcher crawled in behind them, bracing his back against the fridge. His face was stark white from the pain, and he pulled his cell phone from his pocket and tossed it to Mason. "Call Tyler. Speed dial two." He then slid into a position between them and the back door and drew his gun, propping it on his knees.

Mason fumbled with the phone, finally getting it

open and dialed. When Tyler answered, words tumbled out of Mason in a confusion of French and English, which, amazingly, Tyler understood. His only response was, "Hang on. We're almost there."

FIFTEEN

"They're on their way," Mason announced. His face was now almost as pale as Fletcher's, and he dropped the phone to the floor. Karen grabbed a dish towel from the counter and pressed it against his wound, trying to staunch the bleeding on the side of his head. She moved to help Fletcher, but he waved her away, motioning for them to be quiet. They waited, the silence broken only by Fletcher's labored, pain-filled breaths.

After a few moments they heard heavy footsteps on the sun porch. Fletcher tensed as the back door swung open, but the voice that boomed through the room brought relief to them all.

"Fletcher!" Tyler shouted.

Mason almost laughed in relief as Fletcher called out hoarsely, "Over here. Kitchen."

Tyler rushed to them, checked their wounds and draped his jacket around Fletcher's chest. "Don't want you going into shock," he muttered.

"Help me up," Fletcher responded, his words thick and slightly slurred.

"No dice, buddy," Tyler cautioned. "You sit. The EMTs are on the way. Is the house clear?"

Fletcher nodded. "So it worked?"

Tyler paused, then glanced briefly at Mason and Karen. "Yes. You called it perfectly."

A sound burst from Karen that was half sob, half moan as she realized what they meant. "Shane?"

Fletcher's chin dropped as he peered at her. "You knew?"

"No." Tears dropped from the corners of her eyes, but she brushed them away. "Not till this morning. I saw…" She looked up at Mason. "I saw it in the clay. Then here." She motioned around the kitchen. "Also, at the farmhouse I could remember someone arguing with my mother. Tall, wearing green." She touched a strand of her hair. "With the white streaks."

Mason looked confused, and he took the towel from Karen to hold it himself. "But Shane's bald."

Tyler shook his head. "Only since he was a senior in high school, when he started shaving his head. We thought he did that because his black hair had started turning gray in his late teens." He pointed to his temple. "Here, in two patches. It's a Steen family trait to turn gray early, but not usually in such a distinctive manner. Almost no one remembers him like that."

"I certainly didn't. There are no pictures of him like that at the house." She paused, the pieces falling into place. "That's why you took the photo album this morning! To compare photos with my vases!"

Tyler nodded. "The only two existing pictures of Shane with his hair streaked are in the photo album Jake gave you. I'm sure he's destroyed any his mother might have had." He turned to look behind him, where

EMTs bustled through the back door with gurneys. "We'll talk later. Let's get everyone taken care of."

Karen and Tyler stood in the living room, watching as the EMTs handled the basic triage on Mason and Fletcher. Although both wanted to walk, the medics insisted they use the gurneys.

Karen's sense of relief was palpable, as if a ton of granite had been lifted from her back. She followed them out, pausing to look around at the flurry of law-enforcement activity. Two patrol cars had pulled into the backyard, and she spotted the four officers at the edge of the woods. Three more brushed by her and into the house, followed by a crime scene specialist. "I had no idea," she said to Tyler, "that you'd brought out the National Guard."

Tyler smiled gently and put his arm around her protectively, his gaze on the edge of the woods. "I called in the county guys. We took too many chances as it was. It should never have gotten this far."

Karen followed his gaze and saw two more officers emerge from the woods, escorting a handcuffed Shane Abernathy. She broke free of Tyler's grasp and ran toward her cousin, only to have the look on Shane's face stop her cold. His eyes caught hers, and she shuddered at the hatred in his face. Hatred for her.

"Why, Shane?"

He spat on the ground. "Stay away from me!" The two officers jerked him around and loaded him into the car.

"I suspect," Tyler said slowly, "you'll find out that it had something to do with the way your grandmother's will was written."

Karen felt a shade of grief settle over her, mostly for

Evie. Karen had lost parents she barely remembered, but Evie had lost her mother, sister and now her son. "Are these things always about money?"

His arm tightened. "Money or love."

She leaned against him. "Take me to the hospital. I want to be with Mason."

"You got it, kiddo."

For the second time in two days the hospital treated Mason, causing one of the ER docs to jokingly suggest he set up a cot in the waiting room to save time. Mason required twenty-two stitches on the side of his head, but Fletcher's wound required surgery, and they wanted to keep him overnight for observation, despite his protests. He threatened to walk out, until Maggie showed up and ended the argument with a single look.

Tyler, Mason, Karen and Maggie gathered in the surgery waiting room, hands gripping paper cups of bad coffee and peanut butter crackers Karen had bought out of the vending machines in the hospital basement. After a few sips, however, Karen abandoned her coffee on a table next to Mason's chair and settled on a sofa next to Tyler. "You know you have to tell me. You and Fletcher hatched a plan while I was asleep, didn't you?"

Tyler shrugged and leaned back against the cushions. "That is what we do around the office, you know. Take care of folks. It's a major part of our job."

Karen could see the light in his eyes and nudged him with her elbow. "Don't get cute," she said, smiling. "What did you do?"

He cleared his throat. "It was pretty clear that the killer knew you but didn't want to hurt you directly— just everything and everyone around you, to scare you.

We started eliminating everyone you knew, one by one, until only four people remained—Jake, Evie, Shane and Carver Billings. The next step was to establish where they were when the attacks happened. That narrowed it to Shane and Billings. Billings remained at the top of the list until the fire. Although you saw him returning home, Fletcher verified that he'd been at a meeting with a contractor. No time to set the fire."

Mason growled. "And Shane was there last night. Offering to help."

"Probably trying to cover his tracks." Tyler swirled the coffee in the cup, staring a moment into the dark liquid. "Maggie's information about David and Stephanie's will made me realize that we might find a different motive in yet another will—Elizabeth's. Turns out she remained so angry with Evie over her first marriage that she left everything to Stephanie. Elizabeth was dying—no time to win her over. Shane knew that with Stephanie dead, Evie would get the estate, which she did. But we still had no forensic evidence at all to connect him with the attacks on you or the murders. The footprints weren't enough to get a warrant. And we knew as soon as Shane became convinced you'd quit he would disappear...*unless* he thought someone around you would still persist."

Karen stiffened. "So he wasn't shooting at me. He was trying to kill Mason!"

Mason's eyebrows shot up. "Are you serious?"

Tyler nodded. "Yes. We suspect he saw you at the house that morning, digging out those boxes." He glowered at Mason. "God's looking out for you, boy. Shane could have easily taken you out then. Probably thought he might be spotted there, or he would have. I suspect he stayed with you after that." Tyler sat up straight. "When you called from Evie's to let us know you wanted to go to the original crime scene, we realized that he probably would either overhear you or Jake would tell him. He would think it was the perfect setup."

Mason scowled. "You used us as bait."

Tyler's mouth twisted. "A lure, actually. We were supposed to be there before the shooting started. The guys tracking him into the woods lost him for about ten minutes."

Mason was not appeased. "Still an awfully big risk, especially since we didn't know we were taking it."

Maggie tilted her head to one side, looking Mason over carefully. "You already knew you were being watched. And you have to remember something. This wasn't just about catching Shane. It was also about helping Karen."

Karen stood, her voice low. "I need a few minutes." She left the waiting area and walked to the end of the hall. A few doors down on the right, a tiny chapel waited, and she slipped in, letting the door close softly behind her. Surrounded by stained glass and the worshipful silence of the room, Karen knelt near the altar.

"For someone used to hopping about praising You," she whispered, "I sure have turned into a whining slug lately, haven't I? Three days of turmoil. I feel as if I've spent them in a cement mixer. And I still don't know what I'm going to do!" She paused. "But You were there, weren't You? In my friends. My family. Thank You for that." She sighed. "Help Evie, please. And Shane. Help me understand. Be with Fletcher and Maggie. Show me where to go from here."

With that, Karen closed her eyes, opened her heart and waited. Images flashed through her mind, much as they had at the farmhouse and the murder scene, only this time the lace curtain had lifted. The tire swing, the little girl dancing in the yard with her mother, the workshop…only, the workshop wasn't for woodworking….

The clay. Mason. And Jake's words, once again: "Listen to Him. Listen to the clay."

The images brightened again, then faded away entirely.

Karen opened her eyes, her vision blurred from the tears that seeped from the corners of her eyes. They weren't tears of grief or sadness. They were tears of hope.

EPILOGUE

Lot 43

Carver Billings stood next to Karen, both of them looking up at the newly painted farmhouse. His broad grin was infectious. "Didn't think you could do it, did you?"

Karen laughed. "No, I didn't. And I couldn't have without your help."

"Well, old houses have been my specialty for thirty years. Just because I retired doesn't mean I've lost my touch." He reached out and took her hand. "You know, your father would probably have gotten a kick out of this. He really did think you hung the moon."

Karen squeezed his hand. "Thank you. I appreciate your sharing so much about him with me over the past few weeks."

Carver nodded. "He was a good man…and a good competitor. The best I've ever come up against."

"Which is, of course, why you once tried to sue him."

Carver looked at her, puzzled for a moment, then he laughed. "Ah, yes. That was merely business. I was trying to slow him down." He turned to the house again and sighed. "I do miss the work. I know this is finished, but don't be a stranger."

"Of course not. I'll have an open house in a couple of weeks, and you and Annette had better come. After all, we're virtually neighbors."

"Absolutely." He bent to kiss her cheek, then he headed for the Buick waiting in the drive. With a quick wave, he left, returning the clearing around the house to a comforting quiet disturbed only by songbirds and breezes. Karen took another deep breath, simply enjoying the fruits of six weeks of hard labor.

With her own house in ashes, Karen had moved into the Jackson's Retreat lodge house temporarily. Evie, grief-stricken about her son, had gone into seclusion, barely communicating through Jake. Yet when Jake had suggested she might heal faster if she released Karen's inheritance early, Evie had agreed, and had had him call the lawyers. The court had approved, and a month after Shane's arrest, Karen O'Neill had found that she owned a good portion of the land around Mercer, including a farmhouse untouched for twenty years.

Many prayers later, she had known. This would be her home. She had turned to Carver for advice, and he, in turn, had contacted his inspectors, electricians and renovation experts. The house, now refurbished and modernized, gleamed in the afternoon blend of sun and leafy shadows. The logging road and driveway had been plowed and graveled, and the workshop had a new concrete floor, heating and air-conditioning and heavy-duty wiring for her kilns and wheels. And tall windows on the eastern side, for the morning light. Karen had even received her first shipment of Kona coffee, perfect for mornings on the new deck that graced the back of the house.

She turned her face into a beam of sunlight and closed her eyes, feeling more blessed and peaceful than ever. "Thank You, God!"

Karen walked up the steps and across the now-sturdy porch, her bare feet padding across the wooden planks. Inside, bright colors, new furniture and comfy pillows and throws had turned the dusty living room into a home again. Lacey, rescued from the vet after the fire, had spent the past few weeks chasing mice and exploring a brand-new set of trees to climb. Now she stretched and meowed at Karen from a sun-drenched rocker near the front window.

Sometimes, Karen still felt she could hear her parents in these rooms. Nothing ghostly or supernatural—just the legacy of a beloved family home. Two pictures of them, gifts from Jake, graced the mantel, and Karen went to them now, shifting each slightly. "Welcome home, Mama. It's ours again, Daddy."

The sound of tires crunching over gravel sent her back to the porch. Surely it was too soon to have company. She grinned at the sight of the familiar red sports car, however, and went to the bottom step to wait for him.

The gash on Mason's head was still an angry scar, and he had cut all of his hair to match the clipped section the doctors had trimmed to stitch the cut closed. A little gel meant he looked more like a lawyer than an adventure-minded professor, which matched his clothes today. He wore a three-piece suit, complete with a silk handkerchief in his pocket.

He was still Mason, however, and Karen laughed

when she spotted the hiking boots on his feet as he got out of the car. He almost tripped in his excitement to get to his trunk. "Just wait till you see!" he called out to her. He pulled out a large box and crossed the yard with it, with a grin on his face almost as big as the box.

"How was the trip?" she asked. "You've been gone for almost a week."

"Research," he answered. "After New York, I detoured to Boston. And look what I found at an auction in Boston!" He opened the box, dug through the thick packing and emerged again, cradling a delicate piece of deep blue and emerald-green ceramic in his hands. Karen's breath caught in her throat as she realized three other vases lay in the box.

Four vases. Unique. Creative. Distinctive. Elegant. Yet not the face vases that had haunted her dreams for so many years. No, these were the first four O'Neill vases ever to go on the market. These were the beginning of her career.

Mason couldn't contain his glee. "Remember? You showed me the picture that day in the basement. The first ones you sold. The ones that meant you could really do this for a living. They were up for auction, Lot 43, and, girl, there was a fight for them. But I had to have them. Had to."

Karen stared at him, then the vases, then back at him. Her heart ached to know he cared that much, that he wanted this for her.

"Oh, Mason. I don't know what to say."

He gently placed the vase back in the box and took her hands in his. "Say yes."

Yes? What kind of answer… "I don't understand."

He pulled her closer, and reached up to touch her cheek. "Consider them a wedding present. From the groom to his bride."

Yes.

* * * * *

Dear Reader,

In John 10:10, the Lord promises us, "I came to give life with joy and abundance." Abundance, yes, but nowhere are we promised a life free of troubles and pain. Our faith does not prevent trials; it provides us with the strength and ammunition to persevere through them.

Karen O'Neill has had a lifetime of problems, yet has found strength and comfort in her relationship with God. Mason, whose faith is reserved, finds in Karen an example of how to live openly in God's presence every day.

When we walk with God, we may be the only example of true faith some people ever see. My prayer is that we all find the strength to persevere, thus providing a picture of God's love for everyone around us.

Blessings to you all,

Ramona Richards

A note on the Bible translation: For scripture passages, I have used a new version, *The Voice*. The New Testament will be available in October 2008.

QUESTIONS FOR DISCUSSION

1. Karen tries to begin every day by praising God and thanking Him for her blessings. Even when her world has been turned upside down, she goes to the Lord in prayer. Do you have a similar routine? What does it mean to you?

2. How do you think her reliance on God strengthens Karen through her ordeal? What strength have you ever found through your praise of the Lord?

3. Early in the novel, Mason feels a reluctance to talk about his faith. Have you ever been around people with whom you felt uncomfortable discussing your faith? How did this discomfort affect your relationship with these people?

4. Karen was only seven when her parents died, yet she grew up with a strong role model in the faith (Jake), and many of the people in Mercer considered her a part of the family. What does scripture say about giving comfort and support to other believers, making them like family (see Romans 12:10–12)?

5. As Karen struggles to trust God in her troubles, her nightmares return. Have you ever felt as if God were letting you down or adding to your problems for some reason? How did you work your way through this?

6. In what way have events in your life ever made you question God's wisdom or work in your life?

7. Toward the end, Karen realizes Jake had been guiding her toward answers about her parents instead of always providing them. Have you had mentors in your life who have helped you with your faith and dealing with life's bumps and stumbles?

8. What does scripture say about believers leading each other in the faith (see 1 Timothy 4:12–13; Titus 2:3–5)? What do you think?

9. When others ask you about your faith, what's the first thing to come to your mind? What experiences have you had that could help others in their spiritual growth?

10. Some of the details Karen learns about her parents make her question the impressions she has of them as ethical people. If you have faced a situation that made you question the ethics or behavior of someone you trusted, what actions did you take? How can your faith provide guidance and understanding in such a situation?

11. During her darkest moments, Karen feels compelled to abandon the course she believes God set for her life. We can also face moments when we feel our beliefs and life choices to be under attack. Have you ever contemplated giving up on a goal or decision you believed to be God-ordained?

12. At the end of the book, Karen rebuilds her family home instead of the cottage she'd loved so much. In some ways this means going backward in order to move forward. What situations in your own life have meant taking a step backward in order to heal and find a new direction for a problem or situation? What support for this decision did you find in your faith, your family and your church?

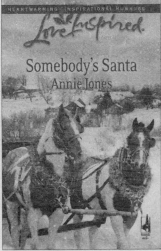

REQUEST YOUR FREE BOOKS!
2 FREE RIVETING INSPIRATIONAL NOVELS
PLUS 2 FREE MYSTERY GIFTS

Love Inspired®
SUSPENSE

YES! Please send me 2 FREE Love Inspired® Suspense novels and my 2 FREE mystery gifts (gifts are worth about $10). After receiving them, if I don't wish to receive any more books, I can return the shipping statement marked "cancel". If I don't cancel, I will receive 4 brand-new novels every month and be billed just $4.24 per book in the U.S. or $4.74 per book in Canada, plus 25¢ shipping and handling per book and applicable taxes, if any*. That's a savings of over 20% off the cover price! I understand that accepting the 2 free books and gifts places me under no obligation to buy anything. I can always return a shipment and cancel at any time. Even if I never buy another book, the two free books and gifts are mine to keep forever.

123 IDN ERXX 323 IDN ERXM

Name	(PLEASE PRINT)	
Address		Apt. #
City	State/Prov.	Zip/Postal Code

Signature (if under 18, a parent or guardian must sign)

Order online at www.LoveInspiredSuspense.com
Or mail to Steeple Hill Reader Service:
IN U.S.A.: P.O. Box 1867, Buffalo, NY 14240-1867
IN CANADA: P.O. Box 609, Fort Erie, Ontario L2A 5X3
Not valid to current subscribers of Love Inspired Suspense books.

Want to try two free books from another series?
Call 1-800-873-8635 or visit www.morefreebooks.com

* Terms and prices subject to change without notice. N.Y. residents add applicable sales tax. Canadian residents will be charged applicable provincial taxes and GST. Offer not valid in Quebec. This offer is limited to one order per household. All orders subject to approval. Credit or debit balances in a customer's account(s) may be offset by any other outstanding balance owed by or to the customer. Please allow 4 to 6 weeks for delivery. Offer available while quantities last.

Your Privacy: Steeple Hill Books is committed to protecting your privacy. Our Privacy Policy is available online at www.SteepleHill.com or upon request from the Reader Service. From time to time we make our lists of customers available to reputable third parties who may have a product or service of interest to you. If you would prefer we not share your name and address, please check here. ☐

LISUS08R

Love Inspired®
SUSPENSE

TITLES AVAILABLE NEXT MONTH
Don't miss these four stories in October

FORSAKEN CANYON by Margaret Daley

Kit Sinclair is determined to hike through Desolation Canyon. Tribal chief of police Hawke Lonechief can't stop her, so he agrees to lead her—on *his* terms. Hawke knows the dangers the canyon holds...yet is he prepared for the stalker dogging their steps?

COUNTDOWN TO DEATH by Debby Giusti
Magnolia Medical

Five people have contracted a rare, deadly disease. It's up to medical researcher Allison Stewart to track down the source. Research is one thing—defending her life is another! Handsome recluse Luke Garrison comes to her aid. Still, with the blame for an unsolved murder hanging over Luke's head, Allison might be setting herself up to become victim number six.

A TASTE OF MURDER by Virginia Smith

A beauty pageant judge is murdered—and Jasmine Delaney could be next. She arrived in town for a wedding during the Bar-B-Q festival. But when she fills in as a pageant judge, the bride's brother, Derrick Rogers, fears she's the next target. The killer has had a taste of murder. And is hungry for more.

NOWHERE TO RUN by Valerie Hansen

Her former boyfriend told her to run...so she did. And now the thugs who killed him are after Marie Parnell and her daughter. Stuck with car trouble in Serenity, Arkansas, Marie dares to confide in handsome mechanic Seth Whitfield—who has some secrets of his own.

LISCNM0908